I0645914

THE SNOW GIRL

BOOKS IN THE ARGOSY LIBRARY:

SATAN'S MARK: THE COMPLETE CASES
OF SATAN HALL, VOLUME 2
CARROLL JOHN DALY

INTO AND OUT OF THE PRIMITIVE
ROBERT AMES BENNET

THE WEB OF DESTINY: THE COMPLETE
CABALISTIC CASES OF SEMI DUAL, VOLUME 4
J.U. GIESY & JUNIUS B. SMITH

MIDNIGHT TAXI: THE COMPLETE CASES
OF SMOOTH KYLE, VOLUME 1
BORDEN CHASE

THE JADE SERPENT: THE COMPLETE CHINATOWN
CASES OF JIMMY WENTWORTH, VOLUME 2
SIDNEY HERSCHEL SMALL

THE SAPPHIRE DEATH: THE ADVENTURES
OF PETER THE BRAZEN, VOLUME 7
LORING BRENT

THE SWAMP ANGEL: THE COMPLETE
CASES OF CALHOUN, VOLUME 2
EDWARD PARRISH WARE

STUNT MAN
EUSTACE L. ADAMS

THE DARK PERIL
MAX BRAND

THE SNOW GIRL
RAY CUMMINGS

THE SNOW GIRL

RAY CUMMINGS

ILLUSTRATRATIONS BY
ROGER B. MORRISON

COVER BY
ROBERT A. GRAEF

POPULAR PUBLICATIONS · 2024

© 2024 Popular Publications, an imprint of Steeger Properties, LLC

First Edition—2024

PUBLISHING HISTORY

"The Snow Girl" originally appeared in the November 2–23, 1929 issues of *Argosy* magazine (Vol. 207, No. 5–Vol. 208, No. 2). Copyright © 1929 by The Frank A. Munsey Company. Copyright renewed © 1956, 1957 and assigned to Steeger Properties, LLC. All rights reserved.

"About the Author" originally appeared in the September 1940 issue of *Fantastic Novels* magazine. Copyright © 1940 Popular Publications, Inc. Copyright renewed © 1967 and reassigned to Steeger Properties, LLC. All rights reserved.

ALL RIGHTS RESERVED

No part of this book may be reproduced or utilized in any form or by any means without permission in writing from the publisher.

Visit argosymagazine.com for more books like this.

TABLE OF CONTENTS

THE SNOW GIRL

*Last of the unexplored continents, snow-
hound Antarctica held strange mysteries for
the intrepid men who braved its blizzards,
the South Pole flyers Welch and Dragon*

"Frozen beauty, untouched by the warming sun:
Maiden carved in marble. Is she to be wooed?
Is she to be won?

1

THE BLIZZARD FROM THE POLE

THE BLIZZARD SWEPT down from the Pole on the night of July 3. It began in early evening, wholly without warning. We had had a clear, purple sky, star strewn. White, cold and brilliant were the stars as seen from this ten-thousand-foot altitude beyond the Great Ice Barrier. There was no wind. The temperature was twenty-four below Fahrenheit. Then all in a moment the blizzard was upon us. A blast of wind, unheralded. A slanting whirl of snow.

It was 9.15 P.M. We used Greenwich time, here at the Plateau Station. The schedule of the newly established Transpolar Line was clocked with Greenwich; it had been official now for five years for all air traffic. By nine thirty the accursed blizzard was roaring in a way that in my first winter here I had thought romantic. This was not one of the freak "blue blizzards," which, since they were first observed in 1955, had been an enigma outstanding even among the many freaks of Antarctic weather. This was not one of those, but an old-fashioned one, what we called a "hell-roarer."

There is a fearsome aspect to an Antarctic blizzard; I think beyond all other threats of nature it is the most awe inspiring. In the summer daylight it is bad enough; a drift of snow so dense that the daylight comes dully through; a mad blast whirling at a hundred miles an hour.

In the winter it is incredibly worse: infuriated elements in the darkness of the polar night. The world is a void, grisly and appalling, with the stabbing, freezing blast of death roaring like a mad monster run amuck, eager for something human to devour.

I sat with David Dragon this night of July 3, in our instrument room, listening to the howl of the storm. We were snug enough. There was nothing to fear. Yet the blizzard of the South Pole has a menace inescapable.

David cursed. "This thing will bury us if it keeps on. We should have a decent system of tunnels, Joe."

"I would. Give the men something to do. They're getting fat and lazy anyway."

WE HAD SOME forty men here at the station, a rough but good-natured crew. Three were married, and had their wives here. What a life for a woman! Several of the older men had had polar experience with the old-time exploring expeditions of twenty or thirty years past, just when the airplane was changing everything. We had them, with their rough and ready scientific knowledge; and a corps of mechanicians and ex-flyers. And the all-important cook and his helpers.

There was little to do. The Transpolar liner went through only once a fortnight; sometimes it did not even stop.

We always kept supplies here: food, fuel, and a well-equipped machine shop; half a dozen small emergency planes; dogs and sleds and a motor tank sled which was supposed to be marvelous, but in reality wasn't worth a damn in weather like this.

*A cluster of strange white shapes swarmed
over his struggling figure*

We were some three hundred miles from the Pole. There
was, just established this year, a station similar to ours
at the South Pole itself; and another at Little America
on the Ross Sea, at the Bay of Whales near the edge of
the Barrier. This was all territory belonging to the United
States of America. The transcontinental trail was built with
American capital, and the airline was financed by American millionaires, but it was government operated, as was
nearly everything here in Antarctica.

A wild desolation, this Antarctic Continent; even now
much of it was unknown. Naked rock, with a permanent
mantle of ice and snow. Rivers and inland seas that never
thawed; mountains massed with ice; congealed volcanos.
It was a dead land, the home of the blizzard.

A continent of four million six hundred thousand square
miles—as large as the United States and Mexico—it lay
here astride of the South Pole, in general shape not unlike
that of South America. Its coast was all explored and

charted. But its vast interior, its great reaches of plateau, and its tumbled mountain passes were, most of them, as unknown to-day as in the bygone times when Scott and Amundsen struggled here and Byrd founded the first permanent settlement of Little America.

The Polar airline, in the maintenance of which we were a link, came from Dunedin, New Zealand, crossed the Ross Sea, passed us, and the Pole, and continued north to Cape Town. It was the only airline over all Antarctica. A hazardous flight at best, and in the winter months, Heaven knows, but little less than foolhardy. Yet the traffic was encouraging; the route, with its New Zealand and African connections, began paying almost from the first. And so far, in twenty odd flights, there had been no disaster.

The liner was not due now until July 10. I recall that this night of July 3, as David and I sat listening to the blizzard, we had no intimation that anything unusual was impending. The blizzard certainly was usual enough. But by ten thirty it was obvious that it was worse than the usual run of them, even for this midwinter season.

"WE'LL BE BURIED," David repeated. He went to one of our windows. We were in a low board room. The roof of the building was no more than fifteen feet above ground. A sturdy frame affair, with its special construction it was almost impervious to wind and cold. The window was high. Looking through its double pane we could just see over the frozen snow level; the flood lights of the landing field showed as a dim vague radiance through the howling white murk.

Buried? If this kept up, within a few hours our cañons of paths between the buildings of the station would be filled. They should have been roofed over into tunnels, as David said.

Our commander had gone on the last trip of the liner to his sick wife in Cape Town. David was in temporary charge of the station. I was radiophone operator. I had been, in my twenty-two years, almost everything incongruous, from mechanic at Bennett Field, New York, to flyer on a local mail route over the New Zealand mountains; student at the Belfast University, and wireless operator of a tanker that took me everywhere. An Irishman; my name, Joe Welch; short, stocky, redheaded, and a scrapper by nature, as David very often reminded me.

"Lucky the ship isn't due to-night," David commented. "One of these times they'll hit into a blizzard like this."

His gesture was expressive of the great air liner flung like a feather into perdition. He stretched his huge, lean length into a chair; picked up a book, yawned and flung it down.

"Hell of a life, Joe."

"Right," I agreed. I prepared to send my eleven o'clock routine report to headquarters in Little America, or to the American Meteorologic Station in Dunedin if I could get them direct.

"Get your statistics, David."

He yawned again and left the room. My best friend, this David Dragon. He was an orphan like myself, but with a far better education than I, and a flair for science as well as adventure. David at this time was twenty-six. A lean, powerful giant of a fellow; crisp, wavy brown hair; a rugged, handsome face, keen blue eyes, and an ability to handle men for all his lazy good nature. A fellow of innate refinement and culture, gone like myself somewhat profane from living so constantly among men.

He came back in a moment; tossed me his scribbled memoranda. "Roaring like forty demons, and the worst is yet to come, Joe. Minus 32 degrees Fahrenheit. Barometer down another two-tenths. Ralston says the anemometer won't register all the wind."

"What's it give?"

"Hundred and thirty-two miles an hour. Nice little breeze. But it actually might be two hundred, Ralston says. It's a wonder somebody wouldn't invent some decent instruments."

He slouched down beside me. The low room shook with a blast of wind. The snow was piled solid now against the window. "Rattle it off, Joe. And if you get Dunedin, or anywhere else in civilization, tell them, with my love, that I damn well wish they were here—and I were there."

I tried for Dunedin on the radiophone, and then on the short wave. But before I got them the near-by operator at Little America cut in, calling me. His voice was tense.

I took the message. My face must have gone white, for David stared at me in astonishment.

"What is it?"

"Clarke. Special flyer coming through to-night."

"The hell there is." He went grim. "Are they crazy?"

"Wait." I took the rest of it. I could not hear Clarke very well, and he seemed hardly able to hear me at all. The interference, due to this accursed blizzard, rattled my head phone like a million tiny drums gone mad. I recall that at first I was annoyed at Clarke. Damn fools to check a ship through on a night like this. If it was forced down—a hundred miles from here say—we'd have a fine chance of getting out to it! But in a moment I was white and shaking, with stark fear striking at me. Helga was on this flyer!

"HELGA?" DAVID GASPED.

"Don't know."

"Tell Clarke to hold it. This is no regular storm!"

"The liner's gone past Clarke. They checked it through; conditions weren't like this down there."

"Tell him to call it back." David was pacing the room with gigantic strides. "Crazy idiot! Hasn't he got communication? Can't he call it back? Where is it, Joe?"

"Just left there. Wait, I can't hear him. Oh, damn this storm!"

I got the full details from Clarke. He had been trying to get me for half an hour. His chief had passed the liner; then tried to recall it as the storm swept down—but could not establish communication.

Clarke's signals died. In this accursed storm everything was uncertain. I tried for him and then gave it up. David stared at me.

"Well?"

"Well, that's all. We're out of business, or Clarke is, or the plane is. Everybody, probably."

Helga coming? Clarke had given me a message from her. Coming here to see David and me on a small flyer, on official business of the United States War Department.

"What's that mean?" David demanded.

I couldn't answer that. It could mean anything. There were some funny international laws here in Antarctica. It is not up to me to criticize them; wiser men than I drafted them. There was no sign of war here, though I will say that from the beginning, the colonization of Antarctica brought a strangely intense rivalry between the nations.

Last of the continents on earth, Antarctica seemed to inspire the world's cupidity. A God-forsaken place to live, but there was undoubtedly tremendous potential wealth here, in the whaling, the fisheries, and the mines. It was the last storehouse of the world's wealth, and its exploration fired every nation into activity. There was Great Britain's clash with Chile in 1943, for instance. That is a matter of history now. And because, by what freak of diplomatic reasoning no one can fathom, the United States chose to consider that the Monroe Doctrine must be enforced even in Antarctica, it brought us into serious dispute with the British. But there was no war; and Chile undoubtedly was wrong anyway.

"War?" David demanded.

"He didn't say war. He said she was coming from the United States War Department."

It might be trouble with the Antarctic natives. Unlike the Eskimos, the nomad Antarcticans seemed hostile. They had a government of a sort, but little was known of it—and no civilized nation had as yet recognized it.

War? But it was all driven from my mind by the realization that Helga was here in this storm. The plane was coming, fighting its way toward us; with luck, Clarke had said, it ought to reach us by 1 A.M.

Luck? If it didn't turn back, or get forced down, with luck it might get through.

David growled. "Why in hell could that fool girl be coming down here, on official business of the War Department?"

There was no room in my thoughts for such a question. I could only envisage the flyer caught in the black polar night in this mad whirl of storm—with Helga aboard.

Helga Johnson, David's friend. Like ourselves, she was another orphan; like us also in her flair for adventure. Her father had been a polar explorer, and, I understood vaguely, an inventor. He had been lost in the Antarctic with the ill-fated Blakely expedition, eight years ago. Helga was a strangely capable, self-reliant girl of twenty, of a sort that only this era of youthful achievement could produce. A good pal, David called her. But she was more than that, infinitely more than that, to me. For though we had never openly spoken of it, we had looked into each other's eyes and knew that some day we would bring to one another the fulfilled romance of all our dreams.

I sat stricken. Helga, caught tonight in the freezing grip of this blizzard!

2

"THIS ENEMY!"

THAT WAS A terrible two hours I put in from eleven to one that night. I did not dare leave my instrument; but something was wrong with it; I couldn't bring in anything. The blizzard howled as badly as ever. The snow was a smother of murk, roaring almost horizontally against our buildings on the wings of a wind well over a hundred miles an hour.

David was all over the place on scores of duties. When we heard that the ship was coming through, he routed out the men. There were some ten long low buildings in the station group. Even in good weather the peaks of their roofs were only a little above the level of the packed snow blanket. Cañon paths connected them. The paths were filled now, and the men wallowed through them. The mess hall, on the southern side, was buried completely in a twenty-foot soft drift, with only its heated chimney sticking up. David got through to it with the electric hand plow. But the opened path was gone again in a moment.

He came into me. His furs were solid with snow, he flung back his parka and stamped.

"What a night. Anything doing, Joe?"

"No."

The cold radiating from him sent a chill over the little

room. I shivered; but it was from fear. "No. Out of business."

"Ralston's got a crew trying to get to the aerial. It may be down—I'm having all the outside connections tested. Do the best I can, Joe."

"If that ship goes down and they try to call us, helpless out there…"

He stood staring at me. "I know. I've got the lights going on the field yet. But you can't tell where it begins or ends—you can barely see the lights at fifty feet."

A man came to my door. "Cook says there's hot coffee ready in the mess if you want it."

"Right, Swenson, thank you. Bring some in here for Welch, and a sandwich. Joe, if we should hear from them—if they're fallen—"

"What would you go out with? The motor sled?"

To go into the open in a storm like this seemed almost suicidal. He did not answer me. He demanded: "What time is it?"

"Twelve thirty."

"By one o'clock, Clarke said. They'll get through, Joe. If it's a government plane it's likely to be pretty airworthy, and skillfully handled. But we've got to keep the lights going."

He turned away. At the door he flung back at me: "Keep at it. If anything's wrong here, we'll fix it—you might bring a call in any time."

Twelve thirty. My coffee arrived, but I barely tasted it. Twelve forty-five. The accursed phone remained dead. In my fancy I could see the plane, with Helga, out there bucking this blast of wind. If they had any sense they'd

descend. But where? How could any plane come down
with even decent safety in that tumbled isolation of ice
crags and glaciers which lay between here and the Barrier?
They wouldn't dare come down. Or if they did? If they slid
into some soft drift, or smashed in some crevice of naked
ice? Lying there to be buried by the new snow in an hour.
Without the radio phone, how could we ever find them?

DAVID POKED HIS head in. "Nothing, Joe?"

"No."

"Your connections are all right. Keep trying. No sign
outside. But the lights are all going and everything's ready.
The beacons on the trail are burning; that would guide
them."

I said vaguely: "Maybe they turned back. Might be back
at Little America by now."

"Yes, true enough. I hope so."

He left me again. One o'clock. Then, after an eternity,
one thirty.

I caught a signal. My heart was smothering me as I went
after it.

From the plane. A distress call! Longitude one hundred
and sixty degrees. Yes, that was fair enough—on the established, lighted course directly between us and the Ross Sea
Station. Then I heard the voice!

"Longitude one hundred and sixty degrees, on the trail.
A beacon near us."

I cursed. Damn fool, why couldn't he tell the latitude?

I shouted into the sender. "Where are you? Latitude
what?"

"Down—this enemy—longitude one hundred and sixty

degrees—latitude about eighty-five degrees, thirty-two minutes."

We were eighty-five degrees, forty minutes! Only a few miles from us!

"Down—brought down by this enemy—help!"

The signals died. I leaped to my feet; rushed off for David. The words were ringing in my head. "Down—brought down by this enemy—help!"

This enemy! That didn't mean the blizzard. Enemy? Who would dare attack a plane bearing the United States mails? Certainly no civilized government. Bandits then. There was rumored to be a band of international outlaws in the mountains of Antarctica. Renegades, escaped criminals from many nations, hiding here, ruling the ignorant natives. There was said to be a "White Chief" of them. There were many tales of him—a sort of super modern Robin Hood, hiding here and calling himself ruler of Antarctica. I had never taken much stock in this; a plane could be lost in a storm, and people with too much imagination would blame it on the outlaws. But now?

"This enemy." Did that mean the White Bandit?

IT WAS INCREDIBLY ominous, out in the blackness of the storm. We did not dare launch a plane; we started north through the surface snow, some twenty of us. With the wind at our backs and the light of the tank in front, the dogs followed in our track docilely enough.

David and I were alone, running with an empty, ballasted sled. My heart held a prayer that it might bring back Helga.

The tank lumbered directly in front of us. We followed the established beacon-lighted trail; it was basically some twenty feet wide, and fairly straight and level, with a hard packed surface at its bottom. There was a smother of new snow on it now. The tank plowed its way through, its motor flinging up a white cloud that gleamed in the tank's searchlight. If it could hold the trail, all right; once off it, the tank was helpless.

We struggled forward for what might have been a mile. The light of the first trail-beacon came into sight in the driving murk ahead of us. The wind ripped and tore at our backs, an incredibly piercing blast; to turn and face it and draw a breath was impossible. It flung us forward. I recall vaguely thinking: "How can we face it to go back?"

We passed the beacon. The tank went into a twenty-foot drift, but got through. We fought our way after it, while the frightened dogs, for all their training, tangled themselves up and all but floundered into the yawning tumbled crags beside us.

Another mile. The trail wound up through a frozen mountain pass with the wind howling like a demon through it and the tank almost buried in the drifts. Then we came out again upon the ice cap of the upper plateau, where the wind caught us full, and the ice was, in places, swept clean as polished marble. A numb, narcotic struggle. I found my thoughts in a dull whirl of chaos. This gray-black whirling void, which was the world, stinging, nipping, biting at me, flinging me about, numbing my senses until it was all dreamlike, confused.

The beacons went past. We had figured that the fallen plane could not be more than ten miles from the station, perhaps even less. "This enemy!" The words echoed through my dulled mind. We were all armed.

David shouted at me; the wind tore at his words and

flung them away; even the roaring of the tank was lost; we could see the blue-yellow spit of its exhaust, but hear nothing. David gestured off into the swirling darkness beside us. But there was nothing to see, and in a moment he stepped from the sled on which he had been riding and wallowed on beside me.

And then the accursed tank went astray and plunged nose down into a crevice. They couldn't back it out. Its crew came ruefully from the cabin and we left it, with its gleaming searchlight slanting drunkenly up into the void.

Another half mile. David shouted suddenly: "Joe, look up there! This is one of the blue blizzards now."

A flash of tiny blue lightning stabbed through the murk of the sky. It was incredibly ominous—weird, almost supernatural. Lightning was rational to a summer thunderstorm of the tropics; but down here in the polar winter night it was uncanny.

There was only one flash.

A beacon came at last in sight to guide us, but we knew that the floundering, frightened dogs could not go much farther. A dozen times we had been off the trail and floundered back again. David and I were leading. He suddenly seized me; we brought the sled to a stop; the sleds behind us came lurching up into a tangle of dogs and men. We huddled in the trail.

WE COULD ALL see it, off to one side in the dull glow of the near-by beacon—the fallen plane. It seemed uninjured. It lay on an ice hummock from which with luck it might even have taken off. The drift snow was piling over it, rounding the sharpness of its outlines.

But there was no sign of any one there. A small cabin light was still burning.

We started forward again. Abreast of the plane we stopped; it was a hundred feet to one side of us.

From somewhere in the howling darkness a moving light showed. I remember my impression that it was large and far away. No! Close and small, a blue spot of light. I suddenly became aware that all around us, as we huddled in the center of the trail, blue spots of light were moving. Then I saw a figure—human—a man!

Instant impressions. We were taken wholly by surprise. An impression of horror at something almost uncanny. Men surrounding us—men out here in this storm who were not dressed in furs, but in a garment of white, like ice, or snow. Ghostly figures—but they were solid enough; one leaped upon me, seized me.

We were all struggling in the grip of them. One of our men fired a shot; then another. I saw the spurts of flame, heard the shots dimly as the wind ripped the sound away.

David was gone from me. Then I saw his huge figure fighting with a cluster of white shapes around him. His automatic spat. One of his assailants fell. But the rest bore him down. I caught a glimpse of a man's face close to mine. His arms were holding me as I fought to get out my automatic.

Something struck me. I staggered. Then fell from another blow. The weight of a man was on me as my senses faded.

3

OUTLAWED ANTARCTICANS

WHEN I RECOVERED consciousness I was lying in a cabin. It seemed to be in movement. I opened my eyes to a dim blue glow. I was lying on something soft and white. The white concave walls of a small room were over me like a vault. There were windows, with a dark blur outside them. A sweep of movement, and I realized that this was the cabin of a large plane in which I was lying.

I shifted to one elbow. My furs were still on me. My head was roaring, but I seemed unhurt. The taste in my mouth and a vague chemical odor clinging to me, made me think that I had been drugged.

A whisper sounded in my ear, David's voice. "Joe."

I rolled over. David was sitting beside me. "They said you'd be all right, Joe. Easy! Don't call out."

I stammered: "Why—what has—"

"You were drugged. They knocked us out. Easy, now, there's a dozen of them within hearing."

The room was chill, and fairly silent save for an outside whirl of wind and a murmuring hum of the motors. I saw an archway leading to another small interior beyond, glowing with cold blue light. The white forms of men moved about in there.

I was fully conscious now. A hand touched my face, lightly as a caress. Helga leaned down over me!

"Joe!"

Helga, safe! I seized her hand; I sat up and found her sitting with David beside me. Helga, not in polar furs, but in a modish blue cloak, with an incongruous aviator's helmet.

David explained quickly. "Took only us alive. Killed all our men, and the crew of Helga's plane."

I sat tense, confused, listening to what they had to tell me. The plane, not unduly in distress from the storm, had been flying low, trying to follow the beacon trail. A blue stab of light had come up, caught it.

"Brought us down," Helga whispered. "We came down, and all in a moment we were set upon, as you were. Our operator stuck to his phone—and then they rushed in, and killed him there."

"They? Who?" I demanded.

"Bandits," whispered David. "Oh, they exist, right enough! The White Bandits!"

We sat whispering in the swaying, blue-lighted cabin. My gaze clung to Helga's solemn, intent face; and then wandered to the archway beyond which the white, ghostly shapes of our captors' were visible. One came to the arch and gazed in at us.

A man's figure, short and heavy set. A white garment clung closely about him; he had a round, bullet head of close-clipped white hair. The light glinted blue on his peering eyes. He turned back into the other room.

I realized that these white garments of our captors were

the Perez insulated fabrics. It was used in the polar zones, particularly by the Latins, who disliked furs.

Helga was whispering: "Get your wits, Joe. They drugged you. Are you all right?"

"Yes. Helga, what—"

David whispered: "She was coming down to study the blue storms, Joe."

I have mentioned that Helga's father had been an inventor. Helga seldom spoke of him. She grew up, with her flair for science, studying meteorology, as her father evidently had before her. And at seventeen she had received a surprisingly responsible position in the United States Meteorological Bureau near Washington.

SHE CUT IN on David now. I listened, amazed at her vehement words. There was a driving energy in the make-up of Helga Johnson.

"The blue storms of Antarctica, Joe, are unnatural."

Unnatural? Heaven knows they seemed so. I had only actually seen one of them—a gray-black cloud, with swinging wind and heavy snowfall, and blue lightning darting through the cloud. Unnatural!

"Not the storms of nature, Joe. Man-made storms! Artificial. They told me I was crazy in Washington when I suggested it two years ago. But they gave me a laboratory and assistants. And last week we made one of the storms in miniature!"

David said: "Here in Antarctica, some one is influencing the weather."

"But who?" I demanded again. "And why?"

"The outlaws; these bandits, wouldn't you say so? The

White Chief—Robin Hood—call him what you will. The Antarcticans, if you like; those fellows."

He gestured to the adjoining cabin. He added:

"Why? Why influence the weather? To keep our nations out of here. Drive us out; keep out our encroaching colonies. This is 1960, Joe. The Indians of North America tried to do it with tomahawks and bows and arrows. But this is 1960."

And I had always sneered at the tales of White Bandits!

I whispered: "But why attack us? Or Helga?"

I understood it, though vaguely, even before she answered. She had discovered the secret of the blue storms.

She said: "I sent you a message, Joe, on the short wave, but you didn't get it. Like a fool, I signed my name and mentioned the blue blizzards. It must have been intercepted. They're after me. Oh, you needn't think we're dealing just with ignorant Antarctic savages. They've got a ruler—a white man of scientific knowledge."

"And the scum of half a dozen nations," David put in. "Escaped criminals. A lot of them are Chileans; or anyway, they speak Spanish."

"And English," said Helga. "That fellow there in the archway speaks Spanish and English—he was in here a while ago."

The white figure was still lurking there, as though trying to overhear us, and watching us. I fumbled for my automatic; it was gone. The fellow in the archway suddenly advanced and stood over us. I saw him now as a man of indeterminate middle age, short and heavy set. The white garment clung close to him. A jacket, and a skirt. The skirt was tight, but it stretched with the movement of his legs.

His feet were encased in white fur shoes. His head of close-clipped black hair was bare; but there was a white hood, thrown back, dangling from his shoulders.

Helga said suddenly: "You're the one who speaks English, aren't you?"

"Yes."

"What are you doing with us?"

He grinned. "You are Helga Johnson. And you are Joseph Welch—and you, David Dragon. We do not make a mistake." He spoke English with a Spanish accent. But he was fluent.

David said: "That's who we are. Who are you? What do you want of us? You're a Chilean, aren't you?"

The man struck his chest. "I am Ramón Margones, Antarctican, as you call our country. Naina ordered me to bring you."

THERE WAS A brief silence. "Why?" demanded Helga. "I suppose you realize you've murdered Americans. You've attacked the flag of the United States."

He did not answer.

"Who is Naina?" I demanded.

"Naina, a white girl, daughter of the White Chief who now is dead."

He gazed down at us contemplatively. The blue light fell full on his face. Swarthy skin; dark eyes; a high-bridged nose; a blue stubble of beard on his heavy jowls. An evil-looking scoundrel.

He said at last: "It is not for you to question me. *Si vosotros queréis—*"

"Talk English," said David.

The bandit grinned again. "You are people of spirit. But you of the red head do not speak?"

I said: "I can speak right enough. You've murdered twenty of our people; how is it you didn't murder us three also?"

He waved that away. *"Sí vosotros queréis*—if you wish to look out of the window—"

"Thanks," said Helga dryly. She stood up. Drawn to her full height, Helga was not over five feet two inches. A compact, sturdy little body, perfect always in health and strength. She fronted the Antarctican. "You think we ought to be afraid of you, but we're not."

"No," he said. "I notice that you are not." He gazed down upon her with an obvious admiration—a look on his face that set my heart pounding. I had cause afterward to recall that look.

David said: "Where are we? You can at least tell us that?"

"We are in the mountains of the Weddell Quadrant."

A region least known to-day of all this vast white continent. The Weddell Mountains, some of our charts called it—a tumbled, mountainous area, lying at a general altitude of fifteen thousand feet; the stormiest, coldest, most inaccessible region remaining upon earth. No nation as yet had claimed it.

Margones added: "You question too freely. We will reach the white valley presently. I will call you."

He turned and left us, grotesque in the white flexible skirt clinging to his legs.

4

PRISONER IN THE CLIFF HOUSE

WE STOOD AT the window. I had opportunity now to notice more of the details of this plane. There was nothing remarkable about it. A Gorgsky body of the triplane model, rather an out-of-date affair now; a huge body of the style most popular in the early 1950s. It seemed in good mechanical condition; the thrum of its muffled motors was dimly audible to us. But in the cabin there were signs of its age—and looking out the glassite window I could see one of the wings, where it had been crudely patched.

I whispered to David and Helga: "Where did they get this ship, do you suppose?"

David shrugged. "Stole it. Years ago, by the look of it."

Helga looked at us. "The Blakely expedition had a plane like this."

"Look outside," David interrupted. "The blue lightning!"

Along the bulging white side of the cabin, up ahead by the motors, a sudden flash of blue light stabbed into the polar night. A silent flash; it was repeated once or twice, then gone. I saw white swirls of vapor rolling sluggishly aside from where it had been—rolling like the white bow-wave from a speeding ship. Liquid air, or something akin to it, congealed by the cold of the blue light-ray.

"That's what brought down our plane," said Helga, "and killed our men when it struck them. This plane is equipped to create the blue storms, Joe. We worked on the principle in a small way in Washington."

"Easy, Helga," David cautioned. It seemed that the fellow Margones was listening to us. Helga changed at once. She said, casually: "How high up are we, can you tell?"

A thousand feet or so below us a white landscape was slipping past. There were peaks of ghostly white mountains down there, a cataclysm of jagged ice peaks; glaciers; darkly white mountain passes, solid with drift snow; or again, an open spread of ice cap plateau; undulating like a storm-swept sea suddenly congealed into frozen immobility; and great valleys, depressed a thousand feet, white-rimmed, gray-black in their depths.

All was ghostly down there as a dream of frozen, silent desolation. I tried to gauge our height and the visible movement of the surface and thus determine our speed. It seemed that we were flying fairly fast; three hundred miles an hour possibly.

We had passed now beyond the region of the blizzard. It was not snowing outside. Leaden clouds swept overhead; but they were broken, and occasionally the brilliant frosty stars showed behind them.

How long we stood silent at the window I cannot say. No more than half an hour, doubtless.

The sky was clearing; the clouds gleaming upon the silent blue-white mountains beneath us. The mountains seemed reaching ever higher. We ourselves were ascending. Twenty thousand feet? I think so. Certainly there were peaks higher than that, in a hugely towering mountain ridge. We swept over it. I saw the heights extending in each direction to the distant purple horizon where the stars hung like fallen gems. Vast sierras, these towering mountains. It seemed that the ridge curved slightly—as though this were some small segment of a huge circle.

WE CROSSED LOW over the heights. On the inner side the mountains dropped sheer, almost perpendicular, down into a gray purple darkness. A caldron here, in depth five thousand feet at least beneath its encircling rim. We could barely see its bottom—a gray-white, almost level spread. It was a huge, circular valley.

"The Valley of Drift-Snow." It is on our present-day charts, with the name the Antarcticans gave it. It's almost level bottom, crossed in a few places by small, ragged uplands, lies at the thirteen-thousand-foot altitude, with a rim of mountain heights towering everywhere some five to ten thousand feet higher.

Helga murmured: "We're descending."

We were slackening and dropping rapidly downward. The blue stabs of light outside were extinguished. A white searchlight showed from the bow of our ship. It swung into the starlight, then downward.

There was a line of ragged broken hills under us, a volcanic-looking region full of pits and craters, congealed with frozen masses of ice and snow.

We dropped in a spiral over a white cañon. Upon its floor I saw human habitations—a little huddled group of domed ice huts, with tunneled paths in the snow pack between them; and a few huts that seemed of timber, miscellaneous driftwood, with skins and furs covering the wooden frames into a semblance of dwelling places.

A forlorn Antarctic settlement. A thousand people or less might be here, ignorant, half savage natives. There are many such groups of nomads in the desolate interior of Antarctica. But this village, we saw at once, was different. There were a few lights here—not tallow or burning oil, but battery lights of the modern Ashtakon storage batteries. And there was this plane we were in—we saw now its landing field, with crude old-fashioned floodlights. Forlorn, but fairly modern. And off to one side was what seemed the entrance to a cavern in the side of the cañon. This was lighted; and as we came nearer I could see figures passing in and out of it.

A strange mixture of broken-down, scientific modernity was mingled here with the savagery of the native Antarctican. A bandit's camp. We saw the same mixture in the people who crowded around the plane when we landed. Men, women and children, most of them the heavy-featured, high cheek-boned, slant-eyed type of natives. They were garbed in polar furs, the women wearing ornamental belts. Mingled with them were others dressed in the Perez white fabric giving insulation against the cold.

They all crowded us, jabbering in the guttural native language. But there was a mixture of English and Spanish with it. And there were some evil-looking fellows like Margones—renegades from South America, doubtless. One of them flung a coarse remark at Helga and plucked at her. I shoved him off.

"Let us alone, damn you!"

Margones waved them away. "Come," he ordered us.

We shoved through the crowd. The Antarcticans were

small people, and so were most of the bandits. David towered like a giant among them.

"This way," said Margones. He led us toward the cave mouth. A man stopped us; an Antarctican. Margones jabbered at him, and he let us pass.

WE ENTERED THE tunnel. The air was at once warmer—stale, but there was a current of it coming out. We went back perhaps a hundred feet. The tunnel opened into a cavern. Lights were here, showing a few stone huts that were built on the cavern floor. We passed them and turned to the wall. Polar dogs crowded around us—there had been some outside, but there seemed many more of them in here. Sleds and other polar equipment were standing about.

"This way," Margones said again.

The perpendicular wall of the cavern had lighted windows in it. A single large dwelling was cut here in the cliff face—a doorway at the bottom; two stories of windows, with a crude wooden balcony at the top story. It looked something like a house of the cliff-dwelling Indians of Arizona and New Mexico.

A guard was at the doorway. We passed him and entered a dimly lighted corridor. Margones pushed us always ahead of him. There had been no opportunity for resistance even if it had been practical, which it was not. We were unarmed; and Margones had what I assumed was a cylinder weapon of the blue-ray. It was clipped to his belt; and in his hand now he flourished a new modern-looking automatic.

The interior of this cliff house was surprisingly spacious. We passed arches giving on interior rooms, all dimly blue-white. Down a narrow flight of steps—ice blocks and stone set in a narrow incline.

The lower corridor was narrow. The air was warmer, and in one place almost fetid.

David said sharply: "Where are you taking us?"

"To wait for Naina," Margones retorted. "She sends for you presently."

He stopped at a door. It was the first metal I had seen, a metallic door set in a metal frame. Margones fumbled at it, pushed it open. He shoved us. David resisted; then yielded with a shrug. A current of fresher air was coming out.

The door clanged behind us; Margones was gone.

We were in a small stone room. A rug of fur was on its floor. Furniture of stone: chairs, a couch, a table with a shaded light.

A man stood by the table. A thin, erect figure dressed in trousers and a shirt of crudely fashioned skins. The light gleamed on his sparse gray hair and his thin face. A prisoner here in this cliff dungeon.

He stood trembling, gazing at us. Then I became aware that it was Helga at whom he was gazing. And that she was standing stricken, staring at him. She had been twelve years old when she had last seen him. Now he gazed at this grown young woman. He stammered: "Why—why, Helga, my little girl—so grown!"

"Father—father dear!"

She ran into the shelter of his trembling, eager arms.

5

WHAT JOHNSON TOLD

IT IS NOT my part to attempt a detailed record of this reunion between Helga and her father. Their emotion was something into which David and I could not intrude. I had always known Helga as a girl of utter self-reliance, with a dominant, purposeful energy characteristic of one far beyond her years. Fearless, with a breezy, direct manner at times almost masculine. Yet she could be tender, too; gently feminine—ah, I had seen that mood, and upon it were built my dreams of what might be for her and me. She sat now beside her father, with her arms around him. They whispered.

I heard him say: "Such a big girl, Helga. Why, you're beautiful. And—you tell me your dear mother is dead... You remembered me all these years, Helga. Tell me, now, more about your mother."

There were tears in Helga's eyes, a catch of sobbing in her voice as she answered him. David and I turned away.

We were here in this room no more than an hour; but many strange things the captive Johnson had to tell us.

The Blakely expedition had been attacked without warning by the bandits. The Antarcticans took only Johnson and five of his companions alive.

"Brought us here," he said. "Eight years is a long time. I have been prisoner."

He spoke with a drab, weary voice; he passed a hand across his eyes, looked up at us and smiled gently. A smile so like Helga's!

"I get confused, talking again to my own people. Five of our men; they have all died since."

I said, "Is this Naina ruler of these people? The fellow that took us spoke of her."

"Yes, she is the ruler. Her father—they called him the White Chief—is dead. And she commands now. Just a girl like you, Helga; a girl hardly as old as you are."

I can only sketch this hour's talk we had with Johnson. A furtiveness was presently upon us. We were all prisoners here, unarmed, behind a barred door. Johnson said one of the bandits undoubtedly was on guard outside, perhaps within hearing.

We spoke softly, guardedly. With the emotion of Helga's unexpected reunion with her father past, we told Johnson all we could of outside conditions. He had been shut off from the world for eight years; that is a long time, here in Antarctica. Eight years had brought many changes.

The members of the Blakely expedition had been found by a rescuing party apparently frozen. One plane was missing, and six of the men. The world called it a disaster; there was no thought then of bandits.

Johnson told us of this "White Chieftain." He was, or had been, an American; a man of sixty-odd. A renegade; a fugitive, perhaps.

Johnson said, "He is dead now—died of heart failure last year. A strange fellow. A man of intelligence and of scientific knowledge. He came down here, gathered the natives together, and became their chief. He hated the United States with a deadly hatred. I'll tell you about that presently."

NAINA WAS HIS daughter; her mother, who had died years ago, was a native woman, strangely white, like an albino. Her father, dying, had bequeathed his hatred of America to his daughter.

"About the blue storms," Helga began. She told her father how, in Washington, she had been able to work out the secret of them. David and I listened, amazed; we found we had known so little of Helga!

When Helga was a child, Johnson had been working on the theories of weather control; he had discovered the blue ray, and Helga, at twelve years old, had known of it. As she grew up she had followed in her father's path, to rediscover what had seemed lost by his death.

He said to David and me, "I had kept it secret, but I had the apparatus with the Blakely expedition. We were going to test it out down here; and then we were captured. This white ruler—he was named Roberts—made me explain its workings. I did that, or he would have killed me. He has used it to make the weather of Antarctica worse than it really is. He has kept many exploring expeditions from this region here. They start this way, but always a blizzard turns them back. Occasionally he made a raid. I suppose he must have known of Helga."

"The White Bandit, we call him," I said. We explained what we knew of the vague tales.

"Yes," said Johnson, "I have heard him say with pride that he was known as the White Bandit. Well, he has kept up a

semblance of government here. He has stolen supplies—
he has just the one airplane, and a radiophone receiving
apparatus. The struggle for existence here—"

He sketched how they had lived: hunting the polar
animals in the summer, stealing food and ammunition
from the colonial settlements, occasionally raiding an
exploring party, appropriating its instruments, supplies,
and equipment. Strange conditions, in the colonization of
a new continent! Only our modern world of 1960 could
produce them.

I said, "And this man Margones, these South Americans?"

Johnson lowered his voice. "They are Chileans." He rose
and went to the door. It was locked on the outside. He
listened, and then came back to us.

He half whispered, "This Margones, of them all, I fear
most. He joined us two years ago, he and about twenty
of his band. The Chilean Antarctic colony of Santiago
Pequeño isn't far from here—only about three hundred
miles."

Chile had a colony stretching to the coast; the principal
settlement was called Santiago Pequeño. Margones and
his fellows had evidently come from there.

"They joined Naina's father," said Johnson. "Protesting
loyalty—but they have no loyalty to any one. A band of
cutthroats." He lowered his voice still further. "There is
gold in the mountains here. I'll tell you presently. But what
I mean, I think Margones figures that Naina may know
where it is. She doesn't; she isn't interested. But I know."

"You?" murmured David.

"Yes. But let's not talk of that now. Margones and his

band are after it. Perhaps there is Chilean capital ready to finance them. If they could locate it, and plant the Chilean flag—"

HE BROKE OFF. He put his thin hands on David's arm; he was so slender and frail a man beside David's powerful figure. He added, "You give me new courage. We've got to escape from here. They'll take you in to Naina presently—"

David burst out, "You've told us a lot, and yet it seems so little! What does Naina want of us?"

Johnson did not know. He said, "She is a strange character, this white girl. Her father was more than a little demented, it seemed to me, obsessed with hatred for his native United States. And Naina, born and brought up here, knows no other emotion; her ruling passion is that of hatred. She's doing what she thinks her dead father would want her to do; and being a woman, she goes to extremes." He smiled. He added slowly, "I think she plans now to attack the United States, through the United States colony here, the village of Little America."

"Attack it?" I gasped.

"Yes. With what she calls her nation—a thousand or fifteen hundred people; that's all there are here, struggling for a bare existence, possessing a few rifles and automatics, not much ammunition, sleds and dogs, and that one airplane."

"But that's crazy," David protested.

"Yes. But she has the blue ray—I had with Blakely about forty hand projectors, and the weather control mechanism, which is in the plane. Crazy to attack a civilized nation? Of course it is! But you'll hear her talk. She's going to drive the

United States out of Antarctica! Well, she might even do that, temporarily. Bring death to Little America."

He stared at us with his somber sunken eyes. "Extraordinary character, this Naina. So beautiful, so young a girl, trained from birth into a warped and twisted humanity. It's just a little pathetic."

A footstep sounded outside the door; a hand was on the lock. Johnson gripped us.

"Margones coming. Say nothing of all this; and be careful—don't anger Naina."

The door was opening. Johnson whispered hurriedly, "Watch your chance. If we can get out of here, get back to civilization— You give me new courage; I have been imprisoned here so long, alone."

Margones came in. He eyed us shrewdly.

"You have been planning how to escape from us? *Verdad?* And telling to each other your troubles? *Bueno!* That is what Naina wanted. It will save her much to explain. She will see you now." He added curtly, "The little girl can stay with you, Johnson. Naina say she is your daughter."

"Yes," said Johnson.

The bandit stood looking down at Helga. She stared up at him, frowning defiance; and again on his face I saw that leer of admiration which made me shudder.

He turned abruptly away; he said, "Come, sénores."

He barred the door upon Helga and her father. He led David and me along the dim corridor; up a winding underground staircase. Along another, larger tunnel passage.

We emerged at last into a cavelike blue-white room; into the presence of Naina. She whom ever afterward I thought of as the Snow Girl. Frozen beauty. Maiden carved in marble. Incredibly beautiful. Incredibly inhuman!

6

PRINCESS OF ANTARCTICA

SHE LAY UPON her couch in a white robe diaphanous as though the cold could not touch her. The couch was of a soft white fabric, with pillows of blue-white, smooth as velvet. It stood upon a small, upraised stone platform. A pale-blue canopy was over it; a soft illumination of blue-white light fell upon the reclining figure, and on trappings that might have graced the throne-room of a fabled Oriental princess.

She raised herself indolently on one elbow as we entered. Margones pushed us forward. He knelt at the steps of the dais, but David and I stood erect, staring. Vision of girlhood, inconceivably beautiful! As Helga Johnson's father had said, she was no more than a girl, this Naina. Twenty years old at the most. A girl, slim but rounded into maturity.

Yet as I stared, and she stared indolently back at us, she seemed unreal. A statue of ice. But not that either, for through the filmy draperies her figure gleamed like cold pink marble. Long, pale-golden hair lay in frozen waves on her breast. A face, chiseled by a sculptor of divine genius into a beauty incredibly perfect.

The illusion broke. She moved the pink marble of her

limbs. A flush of deeper red came to her cheeks. Her sensuous lips parted; her eyes, pale-blue, narrowed, and darkened until they were almost black.

No statue of ice this, but a human girl, hot with anger.

She spoke; a sharp, imperious question. "You do not kneel?"

I said, "No. Should we? Sorry."

I plucked at David. He was standing drawn to his full height. He had thrown back his hood. His lips were parted with fast-surging breath. Young giant, perfection of youthful strength and rugged masculine beauty. He stood gazing with his soul in his eyes, emotion-swept, oblivious of himself. At his sides his great fists were clenched, as though subconsciously he felt that this vision of imperious beauty were a challenge to his manhood.

"David!" I twitched his sleeve. "David, kneel down!"

We knelt together on the step, but David's head was up, and his gaze unwavering.

Naina gestured with a slim, pink-white arm. We stood up.

She said:

"Leave them with me, Margones. Wait outside my door. I will call when I want you."

The bandit turned and went out of the room. He was grinning as though amused at this girl ruler whose whims he was humoring for his own purposes. We sat, as Naina commanded, on the steps at her feet. She had not moved; she still reclined on one elbow, propped by the blue-white cushions, regarding us contemplatively. David was nearest to her, within reach of her hand.

She said, and now her anger was gone and she spoke quietly:

"I put you with Johnson. No doubt he told you my plans."

I hesitated. David said, "Yes, he did."

"Quite so. To save me words. This is the time for action, not words. That little girl who in her radio messages signed herself Helga Johnson—that is his daughter?"

"Yes," said David again.

"I thought so."

SHE REGARDED DAVID impersonally. "You stare at me?" A glint of amusement came into the blue depths of her eyes. "You have the weakness of all men."

Contempt was in her voice—contempt for this passion of men which made woman's beauty a thing of allure. Contempt for love, so remote from her whom obviously it had never touched.

David said abruptly, "What do you want with us?"

She raised her eyebrows. "That little girl Helga knows too much about my blue ray weapons. I shall keep her here as I have kept her father. I was going to send you to Little America, to tell them what they must do."

Her eyes darkened again; upon her whole face lay the dark shadow of her hatred. "Your United States!" She said it with a breathless, smoldering passion. "I have had enough of your nation's insolence. This is my land, not yours."

She checked herself suddenly. "You keep on staring at me, David Dragon! I think now I will not send you with my message, but keep you here with me."

At David's expression, she repeated, "Keep you here with me. Is that so terrible a fate? I will treat you kindly. You will learn to serve me, to be loyal, to love Antarctica and me."

"So you dare disobey me!"

It seemed that David started; I saw that his fists were still clenched. On Naina's face there was a fleeting, sardonic look of amusement.

"Oh. Yes," said David at last, "I see."

Naina added contemplatively as though he had not spoken:

"I think that this little red-headed fellow can take my message. I am going to send you to tell them that they must abandon Little America. Leave it—get out of here, out of my country. You seem intelligent, Joe Welch."

I retorted, "Too intelligent to take any message like that. You don't know what you—"

Her smile stopped me. She made no gesture. A smile of such calm, cold confidence that it seemed almost incredible.

"Perhaps they will be more intelligent than you. If they

yield at once, it would spare them tragedy. I won't have them here!"

The calmness of her voice suddenly broke. "My—my father hated them. I hate them—I won't have them here! You think, and they think, because they are a big, powerful nation that they can defy me. Because I am only the daughter of the White Bandit. They shall see I am more than that. Ruler of Antarctica—and they're on my land. I've had enough of their insolence, you understand?"

It was a wild, half-hysterical outburst. From a man, one would have thought it irrational; but from this girl, knowing what we knew of her—it was, as Johnson had said, a little pathetic. David stood silently staring. I said gently:

"What do you want me to do?"

"I'm going to take you in my airplane to Little America. I will circle overhead and send you down in a volplane. You will tell them that they must darken all their lights as a signal to me that they have yielded. I want them then to abandon the settlement—to leave Antarctica and the stations on the overland trail. I want them all abandoned. I won't have your planes flying over my country."

"Suppose they won't agree to do all that?" I suggested.

"Then I will kill them, drive them out. Just because they are a big nation and I am small, I won't tolerate their insolence!"

I THINK THAT in spite of myself, there may have been amusement in my eyes. Or perhaps it was pity. Whatever it was, I think that she saw it. And there must have sprung within her the desire to show us her power. She called suddenly:

"Margones!"

He stood in the doorway behind us.

"*Señorita?*"

"That fellow who disobeyed me yesterday, and whom I promised punishment—have they brought him?"

"I think so, *señorita*. I will see."

Margones bowed with a graceful, sweeping gesture. His ironic eyes met mine; and I felt it was he whom we had to fear, far more than this headstrong girl. He said deferentially,

"May I suggest a thing, *señorita?*"

"What is it? Speak out."

"I have heard what you say to these Americanos. I think I would not make war upon these Yankee pigs—not just now. There is a thing better that we can do." He ignored her flush of anger. "May I lock them up now and talk to you, alone?"

She repeated impatiently, "What is it? They can hear—I have nothing to hide."

"True," he said. "Well, it is this. I think that this girl Helga Johnson is very important in Washington. If you send this Joe Welch to Little America to tell them we are holding her here, that we will kill her unless they send us much gold, it might be arranged, *señorita*. She is official in Washington, you told me so. She does the government work. If we tell them that the White Bandit is holding her, they perhaps pay the ransom. A good ransom, in gold— and food and equipment also. Then if as you say she is dangerous to you, we kill her just the same, and make war upon the Yankees."

She demanded calmly, "Gold? What use have I for gold?"

"It is very nice to have, *señorita*." He bowed again, and

flung David and me his ironic glance. "If we demand both food and gold, you and your people take the food—and me and my men, yes, we are satisfied with the gold."

She waved him away. "You annoy me with such plans. I will ask nothing of the Americans. Bring me that disobedient fellow for his punishment."

Margones assented. *"Sí, señorita;* I obey."

He left us. Swift thoughts leaped at me. We were alone, here in this cave room. Its white draperies of fabric shrouded windows quite near us. They were open. I glanced at one out of the tail of my eye. It seemed that we were perhaps thirty feet above the level of the cavern floor outside. Swift thoughts. If we could escape from here—

Naina moved. She sat up abruptly. Her feet came from the couch to the step beside us, feet of pink-white marble, incased in sandals. The soft fabric of her robe brushed me, and I became aware of a perfume from it—a perfume which had all this time enveloped us, but was now more intense. A wave of it flowed out, exotically alluring; yet I knew that a little more might steal my senses. In her hand, as it hung idly at her side, was a small white cylinder. A perceptible cold radiated from it.

She said quietly, "You think you might escape from me? Don't try it." She added, after a moment of silence, "I will show you what punishment is—what comes to those who dare disobey me.

"My people love me; but they know I am master. I treat them kindly when they do right, and I bring swift justice to those who do wrong. Ah, you have him, Margones?"

THE BANDIT HAD already returned. There was a commotion at the door. Several Antarticans stood there waiting as Margones brought in the culprit.

Naina commanded, "Stand away, you two. You shall see now how my father taught me to rule."

I drew David aside; he was still standing staring, as though fascinated. Margones came toward us, pushing a chattering, terrified wretch before him, a small, slender Antartican native man. He wore trousers of animal skin; from the waist up he was stripped. When Margones released him he fell to the floor. Naina drew herself to her full height, gazing down imperiously upon him as he groveled at her feet. He chattered, mumbling in the native language.

"Speak English," she commanded. "I want these Americans to hear you, to see how I treat those who disobey me."

"Princess, have mercy!"

"Did you steal one of my cylinders of the blue ray—and a rifle, and the sled and dog of Umo?"

"Princess, I did."

"And were gone with them for a day?"

"Princess, my woman she is with another child. I wanted something good for her to eat. She is sick so much. I thought if I kill an animal—"

"In the winter night?"

"I thought I might. She thought if she eat some liver— Our food is so much the same—you have given us no liver for so long, princess. My woman she sick from the seal meat now, she cannot eat like the rest of us."

"I give you all good food. You knew it was forbidden for you to leave the camp?"

"Princess, yes! But I wanted—I thought—"

"And you did leave the camp?"

"Yes, but I—"

"Enough. You broke my law. You did it knowingly. You admit that?"

"Princess, yes. But—"

"Enough. You are guilty."

She stood like a statue of ice gazing down at him. Her cold white beauty was inhuman. She seemed not angry now, but white, calm and quiet. Judicial.

I gasped, "What are you going to do?"

"Be still!" snapped Margones.

At my words Naina turned and flashed me a glance. "Punish him as I would punish you for disobedience." From the couch behind her she picked up a metal handle from which dangled a length of wire. Like a long whip she lashed it tentatively in the air.

The wretch at her feet screamed, "No, princess, no!"

Abruptly David leaped forward.

"Stand back!" rasped Naina.

But he did not. Instead, he seized her by the shoulders. There was a flurry behind us where the Antarcticans stood watching in the doorway. Beside me, Margones took a step; an automatic was in his hand.

But Naina's gesture waved him off. "You!" She gasped her astonishment. David's bulk towered head and shoulders above her; she was slim and small as a child beside him.

He stood gripping her, and she gazed up into his face. **"YOU DARE TO** touch me!" She found her voice.

Her hand upraised warned Margones back. She was rigid, blazing at David; but his grasp did not relax.

I muttered, "David—"

But he did not heed me.

"Punish him," he said, "some other way. If you have to punish him."

Their glances crossed like swords. And it seemed for an instant that his will was stronger.

She gasped, "You—you are hurting me."

He dropped his hands at once. "I'm sorry. I did not mean to hurt you. There's no need to punish him. He hasn't done anything wrong."

"Hasn't he?" A fury swept her, and I knew that David had lost. "Stand away from me! Margones, take him—"

I warned sharply, "David!"

Margones and I pulled at him. He stood a head taller than either of us. As David resisted, the bandit hissed, "You fool, do you want death?"

"Easy, David!" I drew him aside. "You can't do anything."

We stood watching. Naina lashed the wire again. A current hummed in it so that it glowed with a vivid blue light.

David and I, even six feet away, could feel its stinging cold as Naina lashed it back and forth.

"Stand up!" she commanded.

But the wretch could not stand. He tried, but his shaking knees gave way. He groveled, whimpered, chattering with terror.

And then she struck him. The wire had the sting of a steel whip; its terrible cold burned his flesh like fire. He screamed, and she lashed again.

"So you would dare disobey me!" She wound it around

one of his arms, held it an instant, and jerked it away. The mark of it showed on his blackened, frozen flesh.

"Princess! Mercy! Have mercy!"

"Why? Why should I?"

"Princess! *Aie,* stop!"

A white mist was swirling around us. Through it the white, beautiful figure of Naina showed like an avenging fury, lashing.

The blue fire of the whip gleamed through the mist.

"Disobedient servant!"

The fellow's screams, the hiss of the wire, the snapping radiations of the frigid air, mingled in a confusion of horror. Snow in tiny, dustlike particles was falling in the room.

David jerked away from Margones.

"Naina, stop!"

The whip caught David a glancing, stinging blow. Naina held it motionless. She fronted David. Her white breast was heaving with her exertion, but she smiled calmly.

"Stand back. You are in my way."

"No!" gasped David. "Stop this. Don't torture him."

"Stand back."

"No!" David reached for the whip.

Margones was grinning. "Shall I shoot him, *señorita?*"

"No." She eyed David calmly. "You, too, would disobey me?"

"Yes. You can't do this."

"And why not?"

"Because it's—inhuman."

"Inhuman?" She laughed. "Inhuman? What is that? This is punishment, discipline. It is what you will deserve if you annoy me further."

He said slowly, "I will not let you go on with this. I tell you to stop."

Again they crossed glances. It may have been that she felt his challenge; perhaps it held a lure for her. But she stared at him calmly.

"Stand back."

"No!"

David lost again. Angry color mounted the slender white column of her throat; her eyes flashed.

"No man dares disobey me!"

"But I dare. Give me that whip."

She lashed it at David. And as he fought to take it away from her she suddenly struck him on the head with the heavy metal handle of the whip. He fell. Margones shoved the automatic against me as I started forward. "Don't move! *Dios!* What a fool is your friend!"

The Antarcticans in the doorway came rushing forward. I was seized and jerked from the room.

The last I saw was David lying there beside the groveling wretch. Margones was grinning. And Naina stood there, gazing down at David—gazing in mute surprise at what she had done.

7

THE CONFERENCE IN
LITTLE AMERICA

THE GOVERNOR'S SECRETARY sneered.

"A somewhat fantastic story, you'll admit that, eh?"

"Yes," I agreed.

"And what are we to do; believe it?"

"I don't know; I'm telling you the truth. Believe what you like."

"We're supposed to get excited over it, eh? I'm to rush to Governor Bland with this horrible news that the United States is about to be driven out of Antarctica. And he'll radio to the President, and he'll decide that we've had war declared on us and we'd better surrender. Is that it? The Washington officials will say you're looking for personal publicity. Hope the newscasters will play you up."

I mopped my forehead. It was oppressively hot in Secretary Rankin's office in the Administration Building of Little America. Through the double windows the lights of the main street gleamed yellow on the packed snow. The time was 9 P.M. Greenwich, July 5, 1960. The governor was playing cards with some friends. My story wasn't important enough to interrupt him.

Rankin said, "To-morrow night at this time we're

supposed to dim all our lights as a signal we've surren-
dered?"

"Yes," I said. "That's what I was told to tell you."

"And then decamp? Evacuate the city? Wouldn't that be
a nice job, to rout out five thousand people in the middle
of this hellish polar winter! Do what with them? March
them out over the Ice Barrier?"

"I've told you all I know," I protested.

"How will this bandit's daughter know whether we dim
our lights tomorrow night or not?"

"She'll be circling overhead in her aero."

"Like you did awhile ago?" Rankin demanded sarcas-
tically.

"Yes."

"Well, if her plane was up there tonight, our lookouts
didn't see it."

He was exasperating. "Don't be a fool," I retorted. "I
volplaned down, didn't I?"

The little winged board—a volplane of the old type—
had brought me down from Naina's plane. I had landed
alone on the Little America field. Naina had sent me at
once on her mission. The weather was propitious; the trip
had taken only a few hours. There was no one on the plane
whom I knew. Some were Margones's men, but most of
the crew were native Antarcticans. I had not seen Helga or
David again. Naina came to start me off. She assured me
that David was not seriously hurt. She added:

"You may think to advise your country to try and send a
warplane here against me. Don't do it! I warn you, don't!"

"Why not?" I demanded.

"It will never reach here. I will turn it back with high

winds or a blizzard. And if it makes the attempt, I will kill this Helga and David, and Johnson too."

She stared at me with her smoldering eyes. "Do you believe me?"

I did indeed. And now, talking with Rankin, I suppressed my instinct to suggest that an expedition be sent to locate this bandit camp and rescue the American prisoners.

I repeated, "I volplaned down, didn't I? You don't suppose I dropped from heaven?"

He smiled at that. "I believe your story, Welch. But this weather control part stumps me. Daughter of the White Bandit, sailing over Little America tonight—all right. I have to believe it. But why didn't we see the plane?"

"Because its weather-control apparatus threw a dark-gray cloud under it like a smoke screen. You saw that cloud, didn't you?"

"Yes," he admitted. "Looked like one of those damned blue storms, but it didn't materialize."

"You saw the blue flashes? Your weather was disturbed? Crazy switching winds?"

As he nodded, I added, "Well, there is nothing mysterious in it. If poor Blakely or any of his men were here, they'd tell you all about it. They had it with their expedition; Johnson is the only one of them left alive."

RANKIN WAS CONVINCED at last. "But look here," he said, "we'll put this up to the governor. What would you advise us to do? He'll do what you say, short of taking the threat of an outlaw too seriously. Shall we get a warplane to fly down from Dunedin and try and locate this bandit camp?"

"No!" I exclaimed.

"Why not?"

I told him why.

"Well, then, we'll have to wait and see what she does to us."

"You couldn't get the warplane anyway," I said. "The red tape at Washington would hold it up two or three days."

I could imagine us trying to explain this bandit threat to the stodgy Washington officials!

Rankin said, "You're right on that. Whatever she does will happen tomorrow night. Look here, what will she do to us? A hell-raising blue blizzard? We can weather it. Listen: how will she know whether we dim our lights or not?"

"I told you she'd be overhead."

"Yes, but if she's above that liquid air cloud?"

"She might let down a television finder," I suggested.

"Has she got that apparatus, too?"

"I suppose so. Every raid of the White Bandit gave him something."

Rankin thought a moment. "Has she got a radiophone? Why don't we open communication with her?"

"She can receive," I said. "I don't know about her sending. You might try."

We tried it later that night. There was no result. "If she can receive," said Rankin, "she could certainly go to the nearest cache and answer us."

In the old days, I have read, in the Cordilleras between Chile and the Argentine, there were little houses built on the mountain trails. A sort of "travelers' rest." The idea had been adopted in modernized fashion here in Antarctica. In many parts of the different colonies, and in the unclaimed regions, stone shelters were erected. Food and fuel were cached in them; and there was always a radiophone. It often got out of working order; and the White Bandit, no doubt, or other bands of the nomadic natives, had systematically taken the supplies from some of them. But there were still many such caches, "shelter stations" for any one in distress, located in the isolated mountain sections.

"You suppose there's one near this bandit camp?" Rankin asked. "Just where is the bandit camp?"

I could not tell him that, beyond that it was supposed to be within a few hundred miles of the Chilean colonial city of Santiago Pequeño.

We argued all that evening. The governor, when we went to him, was interested and frankly skeptical.

"It sounds as though you were inclined to exaggeration, Welch—not to say hysteria. But I'll admit your story weaves into the known facts."

"What are the known facts?" I asked.

The governor laid a sheaf of official radio reports before us on his desk.

"Here are the real facts, officially speaking. The Bureau of Meteorology plane that was bringing Helga Johnson south ran into a blizzard, night of July 3. It fell on the trail at the fifth beacon north of your Plateau Station. The bodies of its crew were found, frozen, by a party from the Plateau Station on July 4. That was yesterday. Frozen bodies, you understand; not murdered as you said."

I RECALLED WHAT Johnson had told us: the blue ray froze the bodies of its victims.

"But Helga Johnson," I demanded. "Her body wasn't found?"

"No. She's missing; they haven't found her."

"What about the rescue party my station sent out in the blizzard the night of the 3rd? The one I was with. And David Dragon?"

"It came to grief. The men were found dead, not murdered. Dead, frozen." His face was solemn. The horror of all this was getting to him now; I could see that. He added, "I'm giving you what the official radio reports say. I'll admit, Welch, there's something damn queer about all this."

"Queer? What about Dragon and me?"

"Listed as missing." He shuffled the flimsies. "Your station, Welch, is operating normally. The tank-sled was brought in. Some of your dogs found their way back. The Meteorological Bureau's plane was found to be unharmed. Your boys flew it to the Plateau Station when the storm let up as it did shortly after the tragedy. Rollins is in charge since Dragon was lost. Clarke is sending thirty men from here in Little America to replace the deaths."

He shoved the papers aside. "I'll report to Washington what you say, and if this bandit's daughter or whatever she is makes any demonstration against us, why, that will be something tangible. Something to corroborate your story."

A gray-haired, rugged-faced, dignified old fellow, this Governor Bland. In his day he had been a fighter, used to the wild places of the earth. He smiled at me.

"In a few days, Welch—if there is any demonstration against us—Washington will send a warplane or two for the purpose of quelling what they'll call the 'native uprising.' Meanwhile," he shrugged, "as you doubtless know, beyond the automatics of the city police, and a few miscellaneous arms, the great United States in Colonial Antarctica is in a total state of unpreparedness."

"If the weather is bad," Rankin suggested, "this bandit won't be able to get here in that plane. It couldn't fly in a blizzard. Or could it, Welch?"

There was a touch of sarcasm in his question. I retorted, "Suit yourself. It's no different from any other plane except it's old-fashioned; but it has Johnson's weather-control mechanism."

"Well," said the governor, "I'll get off my report. We'll hope for bad enough weather to keep them away. And when the warplanes come, if the weather isn't too bad for them to get down, we'll see what we can do toward handling this bandit. I believe your story, strange as it sounds, Welch. We'll have to make some plans for releasing these prisoners. You can't tolerate American citizens being held by bandits, you know."

But the weather wasn't bad; on the contrary, it turned, for Antarctica, exceedingly good. July 6, 9 P.M. Greenwich time, approached. It was calm, quiet, with a low temperature not unpleasant; a moonless sky, with the stars blazing gems such as only the heights of Antarctica can reveal.

There is a small tower projecting above the roof of the Administration Building in Little America, a circular room set with many windows. In it, as the hour approached when Naina had ordered us to dim our lights, Governor Bland, Rankin and I sat together waiting. And at five minutes after nine the blue blizzard began.

8

WOMAN INEXPLICABLE

MEANWHILE, IN NAINA'S camp, David came to his senses to find himself lying on a couch in a cell-like cave room, with Naina bending over him. He was confused at first; he could not remember what had happened. But here, close over him, was the vision of beautiful girlhood. He felt the warmth of her against him.

"Naina."

He murmured it. He stirred. Instinctively his arms went out to clasp her. But as he moved, she drew away.

"So you are not dead, David Dragon?"

She was smiling her imperious, ironic smile. David's head was clearing; his senses clarifying. But there remained with him the confused memory of her face as he had seen it when first he opened his eyes. A tenderness? Or a fear upon it—a horror as she sat bending over him, thinking perhaps that she had killed him?

Whatever it was, it had vanished. She repeated calmly:

"I thought you might be dying. Margones said not, and he is more experienced with men who have been struck upon the head than I."

David sat up. There was a lump on his head, and blood

matting his hair. But it seemed only a scalp wound. He smiled, "I guess I'm all right."

He felt stronger in a moment; he sat back against the stone wall which was behind the couch.

"Where are Joe and Helga? How long have I been unconscious?"

"Not long. Margones carried you here. I have sent Joe Welch to Little America."

She sat at the end of the couch, calmly regarding David. "You made me angry—I did not exactly mean to punish you in such a way."

"Thanks," said David dryly. "What are you going to do to me next?"

He saw that there were no windows in the room. The door was partly opened; the white garment of a man standing outside was visible.

"Keep you here," she said. "My plane, which has taken Joe Welch to Little America, will be back soon. Tomorrow night I'm going for their answer. Would you like to go with me?"

"Yes." David's mind was roving upon the possibility of escape; and upon other things also. "Yes," he repeated. He stared at her through a moment of silence, then said earnestly:

"Naina, they won't take your threat very seriously. Don't you know that?"

The red was mounting into her throat. He added hastily, "You plan to fling one of the blue blizzards against Little America. They are used to blizzards. It won't hurt them."

"We shall see."

"Yes, but Naina—" He found himself talking to her as

though she were a headstrong child. "What good can it do you and your people to antagonize America? You're holding Johnson here. He's an American citizen; now that they know you've got him, they won't tolerate it. And Helga is an American."

"I won't hurt you." She smiled scornfully. "Don't be afraid of me."

He went on more vehemently, "Naina, if you'd only see it the other way round! Johnson's weather control apparatus could be of immense value to the world. Rightly used, here in Antarctica—"

"What interest have I in your world? I'll use the blue ray, some day, to benefit Antarctica; when your cursed nation is out of here."

"Why do you hate America so? It's your country, isn't it? Wasn't your father an—"

He checked himself abruptly. Her face had gone white; her eyes smoldered.

"My country? You talk like a fool!"

He reached to touch her, but she flung off his hands. "Naina, tell me."

She jumped to her feet, blazing. "You are impertinent. Stay where you are. I will send food to you. But I want no more talk with you."

"Naina—"

"Be quiet!"

He lowered his voice; he did not move from his position on the couch, but with his intense gaze he tried to hold her. "Is that Margones out there?"

"No," she said.

"Sit down again. I want to talk to you about Margones.

Perhaps you don't understand—I mean you trust him too much. He—"

"I've had enough of you!"

SHE WHIRLED ABOUT, and left the room. The door slammed after her; David heard its bars rasp.

The Antarctican native woman who brought him a meal spoke a little English. She assured him that Helga was safe.

"What is your Naina going to do with her?"

The woman shrugged. "Who say what the Naina do?"

Then Naina came again. She stood in the center of the room, smiling sweetly.

"You are all right now?"

"Yes. Did your plane get back?"

She nodded. "The weather is calm. It made a quick trip. Your friend Welch is in Little America now, giving them my orders."

She calmly regarded him. He had leaped to his feet as she entered.

"I've been waiting for you to come again. Where is Helga?"

"She is quite safe." Her smile was queer. It held irony, a faint contempt for Helga; but something else which David could not quite fathom. She added, "You think you love that Helga Johnson, I suppose. Or is it your friend, that Joe Welch, who loves her? You men must always think you love some woman—that is your weakness."

David said, again lowering his voice, "Margones wanted you to ask a ransom for Helga. You were honorable enough to spurn that. I want to talk to you about Margones. I don't trust him; I'm afraid he—close that door, Naina."

She leaped between him and the door as he moved

toward it. There was a guard in the corridor. She slammed the door. She turned back to David.

"What did you ask me?"

"Nothing. I was going to say, about Margones—"

"You talk as though I were an imbecile. Margones and his Chileans are useful to me. Men are needed here; our life is hard, there is always much work."

"But you trust him."

"I trust no one. Margones never had my plane unless my most loyal men, armed, were with him." She waved it away. "You are a fool." Her mood abruptly changed. She smiled again. "But you interest me; I've never seen a man like you before."

Her words brought a new realization to David. This girl was by heritage intelligent and civilized; educated by her father, with a warped knowledge of civilization, but there were finer instincts within her.

She had lived always in this frozen polar desolation. Antarctican half savages, a few captive explorers, and Chilean bandits—it was all the knowledge she had of men. She had never seen a man like David before.

He stood staring at her.

She added: "I'll take you with me on the trip to-night. We start in a few hours."

"Yes," he agreed. "And Johnson and Helga?"

She frowned. "You are much concerned over that Helga."

David saw the flush on her throat. It set a thrill of fear through him; she might so easily be stirred to harm Helga. He said hastily: "You're wrong. I have no love for her."

"No?"

"No. I'm sure my friend, young Welch, loves her. He has for years."

"But not you?"

"No, of course not."

AS DAVID REITERATED it, a surge of emotion swept him. He laid a hand on the white flesh of Naina's arm. It was warm.

He said unsteadily: "I think it is you I love."

She allowed his hand to stay there. She turned, and her calm gaze searched him.

"So? You think that already?"

"Yes."

"All men think that." A glint of amusement came to the depths of her eyes; and her soft red lips curled with irony. But her breast stirred with her quickened breath. It seemed that perhaps she was experimenting with this emotion. Suddenly David was wildly stirred. He said: "All men can see your beauty as I see it." He dropped his hand, for the amusement on her face had turned to open contempt.

"Hate and love are very close, Naina. Perhaps it is not love I feel, but hate."

"So?"

He stood gazing down at her. His arms were dangling at his sides; he restrained a wild impulse to fling them around her. He said: "You don't want to make me hate you?"

Her breath came fast between parted lips. "I don't care what you feel for me. Why should I?"

"Because—" he began.

"Because it's fear you feel, not hate," she interrupted. "Every one fears me, and that is right; just as they feared my father." She laughed unsteadily. "I shall keep you with me and make you feel it always."

She went hastily to the door. He stood motionless as she opened it.

"Naina—"

She went out and flung the door closed upon him.

9

"WE COULD BE FRIENDS"

HELGA, DURING THOSE hours, had been taken from her father and confined alone in a similar room to David's, with a woman waiting upon her. And just once, Naina came. She sat beside Helga, as she had sat beside David. Helga feared and loathed her.

"What do you want?" Helga demanded.

"So you do not like me to touch you?" Naina said quickly. Helga had drawn back.

"No."

"Well, then, I will not. You're going to ask me if David is safe. He is."

"What do you want with me?" She asked it as David had asked a similar question.

Naina smiled sweetly. "I have promised David a trip. I am waiting for the time to arrive."

"I asked what you wanted of me. You and your father generally killed people unless they could be of use, didn't you?"

"Yes. Why not?"

She asked it with a placid candor incredible, but Helga saw that it was real.

"Why not, indeed?" Helga retorted bitterly. "But you

haven't yet killed my father. I can understand that—he's taught you everything you know."

"I think you exaggerate."

"Perhaps. Well, now you have David Dragon and me. You must think I can be of use to you. How?"

"You are a scientist," said Naina. "Is that true?"

"Yes."

"I understood so. I will tell you frankly; I want your loyalty. When I have driven your United States out of Antarctica, your knowledge will be of use to me. I want to rule my country intelligently. This weather control can be put to good use; I can improve the weather as well as make it bad." She smiled whimsically. "Besides, I have eavesdropped on many radiophone messages in the past year or two. Your activity in Washington was not to my liking. I'd far rather have you here, safe with me."

Helga ignored that. "Have you heard from Joe Welch?"

"He is in Little America. I heard them sending out a call for me a while ago. They would like to talk it over. Hah! They do not know Naina, daughter of the White Bandit. I act, I do not talk."

"You didn't answer them?"

"No. I could not, anyway; I have no sending radiophone."

"You might go to the nearest cache. Is there one near here?"

Naina said: "You seem to think it is your part to ask me questions. I don't want to argue with the United States. I have nothing to say to them beyond my message Joe Welch gave. I will drive them out, or kill them if need be. Why do you stare at me?"

"You seem," said Helga slowly, "perfectly intelligent. But you are not human."

"No?" There was no flush of anger. "Why do you say that?"

"Because you have no regard for human life. You are uncivilized."

It interested Naina. "What do you mean?"

"I mean—" For an instant it struck Helga that she might make this girl understand. But words failed her. She said: "Nothing. You are inhuman, that's all."

"Because I kill?"

"Yes. Your whole conception of humanity."

NAINA WAS OPENLY amused. "Have your nations ever killed one another?"

"Yes."

"And you called it war. Well, this is war. You who are civilized add many fine words to your killing. I do not bother with that. What is necessary, I do."

Helga stammered. "You are a woman, a beautiful girl—such things seem so incongruous, cruel!"

"And you think cruelty, as you call it, should be kept for man? Woman may be very cruel, Helga." Naina stood up. "I rather like you. We will talk again. You have quaint ideas."

Helga was silent. At the door Naina turned. "I would like to have your loyalty. Your help, because you are intelligent." Her smile turned ironical. "If you would let me, I could be your friend."

Helga stared at her. "When are you coming back?"

"I'm going to take David on the flight over Little America. The weather is fortunately very good."

"Will you take me?"

"No."

"Why not?"

It angered Naina. "That is not your affair."

Helga suddenly thought she knew why Naina would not take her on the flight. She said, as though irrelevantly: "You think I'm in love with David Dragon. That's foolish."

Naina's eyes were flashing. "It does not concern me what your emotions are."

"How long will you be gone on this trip?" Helga asked.

"Not long; twelve or fifteen hours."

"Are you going to take Margones, or leave him here?" Like David, Helga most feared Margones.

Naina stood with her hand on the door. "What difference? But I shall leave him here."

"May I stay with my father, then? I have not seen him in eight years. Will you let me stay with him?"

Helga had risen to follow Naina to the door; and she saw, with a leap of her heart, that Margones and two of his men were guarding the passage outside. But they seemed too far away to have overheard her.

She touched Naina. "Will you put me with my father, please?"

"I thought you did not want to touch me?" said Naina scornfully.

"But I do. I—I like you. You said you could be my friend—we could be friends."

They gazed at each other. In most ways they were as far apart as the poles, yet it seemed to Helga, as she gazed at this strange, beautiful girl, that all in a moment the barrier between them might be bridged.

"Before we leave I will put you with your father," said Naina.

As she left, Helga stared silently after her.

A few hours later, with David standing at a distance in the passage, Helga was taken from this cell and led to her father's room. She had no opportunity to speak to David.

At Johnson's door Margones was standing. Naina approached. "I told her she could stay with her father. Johnson, here is your daughter. Guard them well, Margones."

"*Sí, señorita,*" Margones responded. Naina did not see his face, nor did Johnson. But Helga saw it; a grinning leer which struck her cold.

"*Señorita,* you can trust me always."

He shoved Helga into Johnson's room and closed the door upon them.

10

THE BLUE BLIZZARD

"YOU SEE THE lights, David?"

"Yes."

A spot of yellow glow came up over the distant frozen horizon; the lights of Little America. The uplands here at this twelve thousand foot altitude lay purple and black and white, a congealed desolation in the starlight. The overland trail wound back into the mountains, headed for the pole; it showed as a silver ribbon with occasional spots of yellow beacons. The night was cold and still, and the stars blazed in a sky empty of clouds.

David and Naina sat in the cabin adjoining the control room of the plane. It had been a swift trip, a few hours from Naina's isolated camp, down here to the inland edge of the Ice Barrier on the Frozen Plateau.

Naina had been unusually silent. She had paid little attention to the navigation of the plane. There were four navigating Antarcticans in the control room, but David had had no opportunity to observe them closely.

Another native, a squat fellow in white garments, sat hunched in the doorway with an automatic on his knees. Naina had spoken to him in the native language, and then said to David:

"He has my orders to shoot if you make a move to annoy me. You understand, David?"

"I will not annoy you," David said quietly.

The lights of Little America widened and spread at the horizon. Within David was a tumult of emotion.

He said, "You know they won't dim the lights for your threat."

"We shall see."

"Don't do anything foolish, Naina."

It was 8:45 P.M., Greenwich time. The plane was mounting. The thrum of its muffled motors hummed and vibrated in the silent cabin. Naina sat tense.

David moved to touch her. He had tried it several times, but always she had cast him off.

"Let me alone." She flung the guard a warning glance. She added, "David, he might kill you. He has my orders—I would not want him to misunderstand, and shoot you before I could stop him."

David moved away. "They may attack us. They know you're coming—suppose they send up a plane to meet us."

"I'm going high. They won't come up through the black cloud."

They climbed steadily. David could see no other plane. The lights of the little city were closer, and far beneath them now. The checkered outlines of the snow-packed streets were visible; and the great gray-black gash, which was the near-by glacier with a ramp of snow field beside it.

Naina moved to a signal switch. In the adjoining room, David saw a sudden activity. And mingled with the thrum of the motors now came other sounds. The hissing of the weather control mechanism.

David had not been allowed in the plane's control room. But from where he sat now, he could glimpse Johnson's apparatus. An Antarctican was bending over it, operating the mechanism; fluorescent tubes glowing with intensified electronic streams; mirrors with beams of tiny blue light upon them, whirling now; moisture sprayed downward into the atmosphere; vibrations of unknown character darting out. And through the cabin windows, David saw a cold, blue lightning flashing with its tiny stabs.

A cloud of liquid air rolled out and downward from the vessel. The vibrations fed it. The moisture clustered down there into a gathering, falling fog. The altered air pressure brought the wind. The plane swayed and bucked. Then it mounted higher. It steadied.

AFTER A MOMENT, the mechanism was shut off. Silence came again; the blue lightning ceased. The plane was slowly circling close above a gray-black cloud which wholly obscured the landscape beneath. But overhead, the stars were shining clear.

"Almost nine o'clock," Naina murmured. A familiar type of television mirror was on the wall near her and David. It was empty of image. In the control room, David saw two Antarticans with a reel of thin-drawn wire.

They cast out an image-finder—a lens mounted with its Forsyte mechanism in a small metal cylinder. The wire lowered it a few hundred feet down through the cloud, where it hung like a camera gazing down at the city.

"Nine o'clock," murmured Naina. She snapped on the television connections. The mirror brightened. David saw the image of Little America as seen by the dangling lens. The city lights were shining clear. Defiance!

David could not see Naina's face; she was turned away from him. But he heard her voice.

"So they defy me." She stood up suddenly and raised her white arms to the men in the control room. And then David saw her face, grim and white, beautiful, but set with the stamp of her strange, irrational hatred.

"Defy me!"

"Naina—"

She did not heed him. She stood like a barbaric Eastern princess imperiously commanding death to her enemies.

GOVERNOR BLAND, HIS secretary Rankin, and I sat in the tower of the Little America Administration Building. The little city stretched before us, white streets packed high with snow, gleaming with shafts of yellow that slanted out from the windows of the low houses. The Plaza was near by; with its storage buildings and its little church half buried in the drift, and only the spire and the cross showing. Behind it, at the edge of the town, the gray-black gash of the glacier and the Overland Trail winding southward were visible. It all lay wan and serene in the starlight.

Bland said, "A blizzard can't do much to us here. The danger is in the north, where they are unprepared for it."

A blue blizzard! These low dome-roofed houses were built to withstand every hostile threat of nature that the grim Antarctic could fling against them. There was no real danger here. These people of Little America were accustomed to blizzards. There could be no panic. An inconvenience, that is all. But my heart was pounding nevertheless as the hour Naina had designated approached.

"She'll come from the south, won't she?" Rankin questioned.

They stood for a moment, transfixed

I shrugged. "I suppose so."

The stars off to the south bathed the snow and the ramp beside the glacier with their silver sheen. We searched there with our gaze, but nothing showed.

The news of this bandit threat had been kept fairly quiet. The city this evening was busy with its normal activities. These were few indeed throughout the long polar night. The streets now were practically deserted. A line of dogs drawing a sled came down the main street returning from having delivered supplies to the nearest trail station.

A few men loitered at the corner of the Plaza, round, gray figures in their heavy polar furs. I noticed that they were gazing into the southern stars.

Nothing showed. And then we thought we saw a speck off there. A plane? It may have been.

Rankin said, "We should have sent Franck up with a plane to meet her and scare her off."

But the governor shook his head. Bland was too experienced a fighter to trifle with the unknown.

The little speck off there in the southern stars widened. Then we saw that it was not a plane, but a small, conical cloud materializing over the glacier, far up; a small, gray-white cloud hanging there in the starlight. We stared at it silently.

Five minutes passed.

Bland said, "It's almost nine o'clock."

A leaden cloud mass was up there now. It spread over the city, hanging low, obscuring the stars, through it a tiny stab of blue was flickering, like the heat lightning of a summer thunderstorm—a mad enough thought down here in the Antarctic.

Another five minutes.

Bland snapped his watch shut.

"Well," he said, "she knows now that the United States won't surrender to a bandit."

We waited, breathless.

IN THE PLAZA the sled stood with its neglected dogs tangling the harness and its drivers standing staring. The blue lightning had gone from the cloud, but now it came again. The cloud darkened. A wave of white swirling fog rolled down from it—heavy vapor boiling and swirling like steam as it struck the warm air over the city. Warm air? The outdoor temperature this night was about minus 42° F.

It was insufferably hot in the Administration Building tower. Then came the wind. A roaring wind at first, we could hear it sighing around the eaves—a whine. But there was a threat to it. And presently it swung and come the other way with a snarl. A blast shook our tower in a sudden explosive puff.

Rankin exclaimed, "That was—"

It was gone at once. We could feel the chill of it even through the double panes. Down in the Plaza the harnessed dogs were frightened. We saw the men standing there make a sudden run, one way and then another. Lashing the dogs, they mounted the sleigh and vanished down a side street. A swirl of dissipating vapor had come down from the cloud and touched them with its deadly breath. I do not know what the temperature of that white mist may have been; they say now that it can be near minus 200° F. The men said afterward that a mere whiff of it had touched them—an icy touch that burned like fire.

Then came the snow, a solid slanting sheet of tremendous soft white flakes, abnormally, unnaturally large. The wind was from the south. The snow obscured the city lights. It whirled and sucked through the deserted streets; the street lights showed dimly through its white murk.

Then the wind shifted. A crazy wind. It swung from north to south like a wildly swaying pendulum. The snow was crazily tossed. A fount of it struck the Plaza; snow surging like a giant whirlpool—a white geyser spouting into a mounting cascade of flakes. It sucked up the drift-snow from the ground. The naked rock surface showed for a moment, and then was covered as the blanket of white fell back upon it.

The gale was now roaring about our windows, an incredible torrent of sound. Inconceivable was the scene of storm-tossed snow enveloping the snug, compact little city!

I tried to reassure myself that it could not harm us,

this man-made tempest, unless too prolonged. But as the thought came to me, it was denied by actualities. A blast from the north and south simultaneously seemed to collide almost upon us. Our tower shook. Some of its outer windows shattered; there was a rumble, sharp, almost like a thunderclap, as the air rolled back.

Bland gripped me. His face for the first time had a startled fear upon it. "Welch, that could blow us down!"

Rankin muttered, "Look there—"

A vivid blue flash through the murk briefly illumined the city. We saw a distant building—a supply house it proved to be—shattered and broken, collapsed like a child's house of cards under the crazy air pressures of the tossing wind.

"We're lost if this goes on," Bland murmured. But it did not. It was only Naina's effort to show us what a blue blizzard might do. The wind suddenly whirled away and left a dead, ominous calm. The blue lightning vanished.

The snow, in a few minutes more, petered out and ceased falling. The cloud overhead thinned. The stars broke through.

And presently there was a cloudless sky. A still, calm night, quiet and peaceful as before.

We gazed at the city, strangely buried in great masses of drift snow. One street was piled twenty feet high; another swept clean and bare; and that single building lying broken. The sky was empty, save for the brilliant, serene stars.

Naina's plane had gone.

11

MURDER

DAVID SAT STARING at the television mirror in the cabin of Naina's plane. The plane was slowly circling above the cloud. On the mirror from the dangling lens, the storm-tossed city was a blur of gray-white murk.

"Why," said David, "this won't do anything, Naina. It can't hurt them; they're prepared for it."

She did not answer. She sat tensely silent, staring at the mirror.

David's mind flung northward. He saw, as though with prophetic vision, a great northern city—New York City, perhaps, with its towering buildings of masonry and steel; its millions of people. New York City in the summer-time, perhaps. Sweltering in the heat. Not the compact and sturdy polar village of Little America, but the huge beehive that was New York. A cloud in the sky some summer night; a sudden seeming thunderstorm, and then snow! A blizzard with sub-zero temperatures, descending suddenly upon a shirt-sleeved sweltering multitude. What a weapon for modern warfare was this! He envisaged the lurking enemy in the cloud-hidden sky—Chile, perhaps!

His mind swept to Margones. This Chilean bandit had the secret.

"It can't hurt Little America."

But on the mirror he saw in the dim swirling murk the collapse of the storehouse building. Why, this could bring death to every home in Little America!

David rose to his feet. He forgot the guard in the doorway behind them.

"Naina, stop! You have shown them!"

She leaped up. Even with her emotion, she had the presence of mind to gesture to the guard. David took a step and gripped her by the shoulders. The guard stood alert, with weapon upraised, but he did not fire.

David repeated vehemently, "You have done enough; you have shown them!"

She met the challenging gaze, and abruptly he relaxed, for he knew that this time he had won. She drooped under the grip of his fingers.

She murmured, "David, don't. You hurt me."

"Tell your men to stop that storm!" He released her.

She raised her arms. She gave the command. She turned away from David and stood gazing through the window where beneath the ship the blue lightning presently ceased its flashes and the cloud was dissipating.

David sat watching her. For ten minutes or more she did not move. The plane had turned and sped away. The cloud was gone. The serene starlit night was around them.

David said at last, "Naina, come here."

She stood, grim, white, and silent; imperious; lost in her thoughts.

"Naina, come here. Sit with me."

She turned, and on her face was a hint of triumph.

"You saw, David?"

"Yes, I saw."

She sat down by him.

He said presently, "You have shown them. But to what purpose?"

It swept him again, the power of this weapon.

"Naina, you are an American. If your country—if our country had such a weapon as this, for war or for peace—why, Naina, there's no limit to what it could do. Drive away storms instead of make them."

He put out his hand and touched her arm. He added gently, "That would be better, Naina, wouldn't it?"

She allowed his hand to rest there. Her face was turned away from him. He sat very still; and suddenly she shook off his hand and, turning, gestured to the guard to go back from the doorway.

DAVID FOLLOWED HER gesture. When she was back beside him, he touched her again—touched her arm, and then found her hand and clasped it.

The cabin was very silent. Only the thrum of the motors and the occasional voice of one of the men in the adjoining room.

"Naina, why do you hate my country—our country—so much?"

He said it very gently, earnestly. His hand tightened upon hers. He held his breath, afraid that his words would anger her.

But it seemed now as though perhaps the spell of his manhood, his emotion—or the emotion between them, perhaps, surging through their clasped fingers, were at last too strong for her anger.

She said finally, and her voice now was different; softer, more gentle than he had ever heard it before:

"I'll tell you. I had never thought I would tell any one. My father—" A break came to her voice, but she went steadily on: "My father was born an American. That's true. And he would have been, perhaps, a great man in his country. But then they said, one day, that he was a murderer."

David sat very still, listening as she poured it out. Her father had been arrested for murder; she did not know the details, or perhaps now she did not care to tell them. He had been tried and convicted upon evidence largely circumstantial. He had been sent to prison with his appeal denied, and had languished there for ten of the best years of his life.

"But he got away, David. I can't tell you how. He got away—broke from the prison and escaped."

A fugitive! Pursued by the law. A man without a country; living always in the shadow of capture. And he had wandered at last, like so many of his kind, into the new desolation which to him and others like him was the lure of Antarctica.

He was a man of intelligence. Doubtless a born leader, he dominated the Antarctican natives. And so at last he had come to be known as the White Bandit. Obsessed with hatred for his country that had driven him here—

"You mean," said David, "that he was innocent of the crime?"

"Yes. Innocent, and the bungling laws of your United States wrecked him. And then at last he was vindicated."

Ten years ago now, in 1950, some one, some criminal in New York City, had, dying, confessed to the crime for which Naina's father—his name was Roberts—was paying the penalty. He had brought proof beyond the shadow of a doubt.

"Why," exclaimed David, "then he need not have been a fugitive after that. Ten years ago—"

She blazed at him. "But do you think, with his life wrecked by the hardships he had passed through, that he would return then when the announcement reached him. Oh, yes, he could have gone back!

"The newscasters carried it: 'The murderer Roberts was innocent.' But how could that make it up to him? Who seemed sorry that his life had been so terrible? Who did anything but sneer and say: 'Oh, well, it seems that the murderer Roberts was innocent after all!'"

She ended with a vehement, passionate outburst: "It only made him hate them worse, and made me hate them. Do you see? And they sneered at the White Bandit. They didn't know it was my father doing what he could to keep them out of Antarctica. I was born here. My mother was a native here. It was her country, and it became my father's country, and it's my country! And your cursed people come stealing into it, spreading out, taking the land—my land! I won't allow it!"

She stopped. David could find nothing to say. This girl, as Johnson had said, was so pathetic!

He stammered: "Naina, I—" He wanted to say, "I love you. Why, Naina, I said it might be hate, and you said it was fear. But it's love." But he only stammered, "Oh, Naina, you poor girl!"

She drew away from him. "I don't want your pity." The pathos had gone from her face and left it grim again. "Stay where you are, David. I should not have bothered to tell you all that."

SHE LEFT HIM sitting by the empty television mirror, and went into the control room. In a moment the guard came and again stood in the doorway, with his automatic upon David, and his alert eyes watching.

They flew on through the starlit night. One hour more? Or two hours? Beneath the windows the frozen desolate landscape slid past. And David's thoughts were flying, too, thinking of this pathetic girl.

They passed over the familiar valley, the grim frozen mountains. As they neared the camp David's thoughts flew ahead; it seemed that a premonition came to him. Margones!

David recalled what Johnson had said concerning the bandit's possible purpose. There was gold in these mountains; Margones and his band were after it; and Johnson knew where it was.

David had been able to cope with Naina. But now, like a warning, came the realization that Naina was not his dangerous enemy. He must face Margones.

The plane landed on the field by the forlorn little settlement. In the shifting lights David saw the assembled natives. There seemed nothing amiss.

"Are we going inside, Naina—in the cave?"

"Yes."

She avoided explanations to her men. She gave directions concerning the plane.

"Come, David."

She hurried him away, and they entered the cave mouth. There were dogs and men inside. A spot of light showed women before a low stone shelter on the cave floor—a family group huddled there. The women were chewing skins to make boots for their men.

All normal. But David was breathing fast. There seemed none of Margones's band in sight.

"Naina, where should Margones be?"

"I left him guarding Johnson and Helga."

They passed through the lower entrance to Naina's cliff house. She added: "I suppose the officials of Little America will be trying to phone me. I think this time I shall answer them; there is a mountain phone station not so far from here. We will go to my instrument room, David. You have not seen my receiving sets."

"Naina, take me first to Johnson."

They were in the lower corridor. She stopped and eyed him in the bloom of one of the corridor lights.

"You mean, take you to Helga?"

"Yes. Helga and her father. I'm worried."

It came to David that he was more than worried. "I'm afraid that Margones—"

It startled her—his words, or his set, white face.

"All right, we'll go see them first. David, I shall tell them in Little America that my next storm will bring death, wreck the city. I can do it—you saw that building fall."

They went down the stone steps into the lower corridor. They had passed a native or two on the upper level. But it was silent and deserted down below.

They traversed the lower passage, with its glowing, dull illumination and its fetid air. They came to the door of Johnson's cell.

Margones and two or three of his men should have been here.

"Why," said Naina, "what's this? How dare he leave his post?"

No one here. In the silence David seemed to hear his heart pounding. No one here. The cell door was closed. Naina bent to it.

"How dare he—"

The door was unbarred. Had Johnson and Helga broken away and escaped? But in that instant, as Naina rattled the locks and opened the door, David instinctively knew it was not so. With a premonitory chill of horror, he was shivering.

Naina pushed the door open and they went in.

They stood for an instant transfixed. Upon the floor, sprawled face down, lay the motionless body of Johnson.

Helga was gone.

12

IN PURSUIT

JOHNSON WAS DEAD. There was no doubt of it as they knelt over him, David lifted up the body.

"Murdered!"

It was strangely gruesome. There was no blood, no sign of a wound. The body was cold, rigid. The garments were moist; they had been frozen with a film of ice which now was melted in the warmth of the room. The flesh had a blue cast to it.

David rose. "He's taken Helga!"

Naina stood stricken; confused and with a white anger sweeping her. "Why, how dare he?"

David gripped her. "We must go after them in your plane. Has he a plane, Naina? Was there any other plane?"

"No."

They rushed back through the corridor. Naina came to an ascending cross passage, and through a small door David suddenly found himself in the main outer cave room. It was quiet, but Naina's voice echoed through it.

The natives clustered around her. The place was in confusion. They jabbered, but they were all frightened at her anger.

It was exasperating to David, not understanding the

language. He stood for a moment in the midst of the group. Margones and his band had departed, that was obvious. But how long ago? Every moment was precious.

"What do they say?" he demanded. "Come on, we've got to get your plane."

"He and his men left on their sleds. These fools here! Margones told them he was making a trip by my orders. His men slipped away, a few at a time."

"How long ago?"

"I don't know." She gripped a small Antarctican man by the shoulders. She shook him, and he cringed before her, chattering with fright.

"He says they have been gone about two hours."

"Was Helga with them?"

"He thinks so. Some one in a long white cloak and a hood. It must have been Helga. These fools!"

From the cave house doorway a man came running. Naina heard what he had to say.

"What is it?" David demanded again.

"He had heard on the radiophone a message broadcasted for me from Little America, in the native dialect."

She stood bewildered with these swift conflicting happenings. "The United States demands my answer. My three American prisoners must be released or in a few days warplanes will be sent to seek me out. David—"

He waved it away. "Forget that. We've got to catch Margones and release Helga. Shall we take your plane to Little America and get help?" No, that would need too much time. "If this murderer went with sleds, Naina, he'll be leaving a trail in the snowpack. If the weather holds—

if it does not snow—we can follow him with the plane, flying low."

A shot sounded from the open valley outside the cave. Then another.

David and Naina stood listening. A silence fell around them. Then a commotion began, there were more shouts outside.

The plane! Cylinder-weapon in hand, Naina rushed out, with David beside her. The little settlement huddled in the snow was in a turmoil. A sudden fight had taken place at the plane in which Naina and David had arrived a few moments before. Whatever it was, it was over now. There were no more shots.

"Come, David!"

THEY RAN. AT the plane Naina's natives surrounded her. She gasped and turned to David.

Now, for the first time, he saw fear on her face.

"Margones left three or four of his men—my natives killed them when they tried to steal the plane."

They mounted into the control room of the plane. It was crowded with frightened, excited people. The bodies of the Chilean bandits, who had been shot, lay there. One was still alive, but dying.

The control mechanism of the plane was wrecked. The last of the bandits, wounded, had, in a frenzy, torn at it. The electric controls were smashed. It would take hours, perhaps days, to repair them.

To David, it was in a moment obvious what had happened. Margones had murdered Johnson, abducted Helga, and, with his sleds, dogs and most of his band, had departed. But he wanted the plane. He had left some of his men in hiding here to seize it on its arrival and fly it to join him.

David drew Naina away. "Naina, this is no time to get excited. Anger is foolish. We've got to follow them."

"Yes. How dared he! If once I can get these hands on him!"

She stood with David outside the plane. He waved away the natives who crowded around them.

"Naina, what is the swiftest way to follow them? A sled?"

"Yes, a sled! I will take a sled with my fastest dogs—I can overtake him."

"You mean, go alone?"

"Yes. It's the fastest way—I have only seven fast dogs."

"I'll go with you."

"If once I can get my hands on him—how dared he do a thing like this?"

She stood tense, lost in thought. David knew that her dominant emotion was desire for vengeance upon Margones. She had ruled so imperiously; instinctively she felt that she only needed to have Margones within the sound of her voice to reduce him again to subjection.

But David's thoughts were upon practicalities. With the plane wrecked, they were helpless here in this cold, desolate mountain fastness. It seemed best to follow the bandits with a single sled and fast dogs. There were twenty or more men in Margones's band. It would not be feasible to attack them. David would follow them cautiously and watch for a travelers' hut where a radiophone would be available. Margones and his band—whatever their purpose—would locate perhaps in some desolate, hidden spot. David would trail them there, and phone to Little America for help.

But he said none of this to Naina. Instead he exclaimed: "Get your sled ready. Hurry, Naina; your fastest dogs—I'll drive them. Provisions and water, all the equipment, and bring some weapons. Tell your natives we will be gone on a journey of a few days. Get a complete equipment."

"Yes!" she agreed.

"We'll catch him, Naina, if this clear weather holds."

The sled was presently ready. David was enveloped in his furs, which he had not worn for the flight in the plane. Naina was garbed in a long, heavy white cloak and hood. They stood by the sled, with its six dogs harnessed two abreast, and the lead dog in front.

The natives gathered in the gloom of the ragged outskirts of the settlement to see them off. The snowfield was a dim white-purple; the purple, star-strewn sky was cloudless.

"Ready, Naina? You have weapons?"

"Yes."

The sled was piled high with equipment roped to it.

David said, "Have you got an automatic?"

"Yes."

"Give me it."

He held his breath. He and Naina had always, so far, been in the roles of captor and prisoner; enemies, with a barrier between them. He repeated casually, "Give me the automatic."

She hesitated. He added simply, "I am your friend, Naina."

She handed it to him without a word.

David seized the handles of the sled.

"You ride."

"Yes. We start downhill."

In a moment they were away. The dogs ran low to the ground, picking up speed. The packed snow showed a long gentle declivity. David in a moment mounted the sled for the coasting descent. The low white huts flashed by in a blur of movement. Soon they were farther apart; then they were gone.

The descent ended. The pace slackening, David leaped out and ran swiftly beside the sled, urging the animals forward with a long, lashing quirt. An undulating white desolation lay ahead. A trackless waste, pale in the starlight. But David could see now the tracks of the bandits' sleds which they were following.

13

"THE GOLD IS YOURS!"

I MUST REVERT now to that time when Margones shoved Helga into the room with her father.

The bandit said to Naina: "You can trust me always, *señorita*," as he closed the cell door. Helga had seen the leer upon his face. She was frightened, with a cold, shuddering fear; and it was seldom indeed that Helga was frightened at anything.

"Father, dear!"

She threw herself into her father's arms. They stood listening while Margones barred the door. Naina departed.

"Father, I'm afraid of that fellow Margones."

He comforted her, as though she were the little girl of twelve he had always remembered.

"Naina is starting for Little America, Helga?"

"Yes."

"I've been worried about you. Did she treat you kindly?"

"Yes. She said I could stay here with you while they're gone. She took David Dragon with her."

His thin face softened, relaxed. "It will come out all right, Helga. Some day, when we get back from here into God's country—"

Life is very strange. It was given to Johnson to find the

little daughter of his memories grown to a beautiful, capable, intelligent young woman; sitting with him for those few brief hours—and then to have his own life snuffed out.

To Johnson, this daughter must indeed have seemed very beautiful. Helga wore a suit of blue serge. Over it was a long cloak with a hood which dangled at the back. The cloak was a deep navy blue with a vivid red lining, a heavy military-looking cloak. She had worn it on the trip down with a fur coat over it, and an aviator's helmet. The latter were discarded in the other cell, but she wore here into her father's room this blue and red undercloak.

Johnson gazed at her. "You are very beautiful, Helga."

"You like it? In Washington they teased me about it—said it was very vivid." She took it off and laid it aside.

They talked for an hour of two. Then the door opened. Margones was out there. He seemed alone. He had a metal tray in his hand.

"Your food," he said. He came in and put it on the table. He did not look at Helga. He turned and stalked out. The door slammed; they heard the rattle of its bars.

After the meal was over, Johnson, who had been talking in casual fashion, suddenly became furtive. He gazed at the door and lowered his voice.

"Helga, if I shouldn't get out of here alive—"

She flashed a startled glance at him. He smiled. "I've something I must say to you, something I must tell you."

He went quietly to the door and listened, then came back.

"He can't hear us, Helga. Above everything I wouldn't have him hear this. But I must tell you. One of the purposes of Blakely's expedition was prospecting in these mountains. There is gold here; Blakely believed it. The government wanted him to find it and stake it for the United States. More than half the money for his expedition was government money. No one but he and I knew that."

Johnson's voice was vehement and tense. A spot of red burned in each of his thin cheeks. "I've never told any one of this, Helga. Eight years ago—and I'm the only survivor of the Blakely expedition. The gold is mine, Helga! You know the law. Mine and my country's."

"You found it?" she murmured quietly.

"Yes. We found it here in these mountains. Not so very far from here. We found it, only a few hours before the White Bandit captured us. There seemed to be a mountain of it! The outcropping was visible for half a mile along a cliff-face. Nuggets, Helga! Strewn at the bottom of the cliff, as though by an avalanche."

HE SEEMED TALKING against time. As though by some strange intuition the shadow of his impending death now lay upon him; he seemed to sense its nearness.

"That gold is yours, Helga. If I shouldn't live through this, you are my survivor—the last survivor of the Blakely expedition. And I want you to claim it. You know the law— the colonial law for such discoveries here in Antarctica? Or has it been changed?"

"No," she said. "Not changed."

"Well, it would be done like this."

The discussion absorbed them. They had been gazing, one or the other of them, at the cell door constantly. But now they forgot it, staring at each other, tense with this thing they were discussing.

The international law in Antarctica had been ratified

by all the several nations holding possessions in the new continent. The conference had been held in London in 1951. By the terms of the agreement reached, the discovery of any natural wealth in any neutral, unclaimed territory belonged to the country of the discoverer. It was necessary then to plant upon the strike his national flag, and at once to notify the International Claim Office in London. In these days of almost universal government ownership and government exploitation, all the wealth of Antarctica was being developed by government funds.

"This is neutral territory, Helga. It will add a whole new region to Colonial America. It's worth colonizing."

The law said that the nation making the strike must establish and hold a settlement with a certain population. This done, at the end of a year, the other nations recognized the validity of the claim.

To the discoverer, his nation paid a royalty. "Enough to make us fabulously rich, Helga—no doubt of that."

He lowered his voice still further. "There's a radiophone travelers' hut quite near our golden mountain, Helga."

His voice rang with the words. He repeated them. "Our golden mountain! Don't you like the sound of that? It's ours—yours and mine! If we can get out of here—to that phone hut—and send in a call for help to record the strike. Closer, Helga, I want to tell you where it is."

He murmured it to her. He could not tell her how far it was from Naina's camp, but he gave her the latitude and longitude.

She said suddenly, "Father, not so loud! You're talking too loudly!"

With his eagerness he had spoken louder than he realized. His back was to the cell door. Helga faced him. She gazed into his flushed, earnest face.

He reiterated, "It's all for you, Helga. That's what I've had in mind all these years."

Her heart was suddenly pounding. She went cold with fear. In the cell the odor of alcoholite became apparent—that intoxicating perfume which of recent years has been the curse of South America.

Alcoholite wafting in here?

Helga's gaze leaped past her father's shoulder. The cell door was ajar!

"Father!"

The startled exclamation burst from her before she could check it.

"Helga—what—"

He turned with a rasp of his chair to follow her gaze.

They had betrayed themselves.

The cell door, which was open a few inches, swung wider. Margones crouched there, leering, the evidence of his menace written clearly on his face. In that instant, Helga, cold with fear, knew that the bandit had heard them talking of their golden mountain—had heard even its location, perhaps.

HELGA AND HER father leaped to their feet. "What do you want?" Johnson demanded.

Margones advanced, lurching, for he was far from sober. A wave of the intoxicating perfume came with him into the room; a strip of gaudy fabric hung like a handkerchief at his chest; he stopped to sniff at it as he advanced.

"Get out," said Johnson. "You're drunk." His arm swept Helga protectingly behind him.

Margones did not speak, but he snarled, and ripped his cylinder-weapon from his belt. Helga was aware of the stab of blue flame. She felt its frigid blast. It caught her father full in the face. He wavered; mumbled thickly:

"Helga! Run—"

He swung about, clutching at her, with the blue ray on him. A wave of incredible cold, with a thick white mist like a fog rolled at Helga. She staggered; and then her father fell.

The blue light vanished. The fog rolled away. Across the room, Helga saw Margones reeling back against the wall, grinning. She was numb with fright and the deadly cold. At her feet Johnson lay motionless. She sank upon him.

"Father! Father dear!"

Ice was formed upon his face; his blue lips were frozen; his thin garments stiff.

The knowledge that he was dead surged upon her. She sank inert into the black soundlessness of insensibility.

Realization that he had killed Johnson must have sobered Margones. Helga was unconscious only a moment; she recovered to find Margones carrying her along a dim passage.

As she stirred he set her abruptly upon her feet and stood steadying her until she was able to walk.

The corridor was empty. He whispered: "You come quietly. If I have to carry you it will cause comment. If we are stopped, I will kill you—by the blessed Santa Maria, I swear it!" He led her forward. "Can you walk?"

"Yes." She was too confused to dissemble. She took a few steps; strength was coming back to her.

"Come then." He had brought her red and blue cloak

from the cell. He flung it over her shoulders. Over it, he put another cloak of the white fabric, and drew its hood over her head.

"There, that will protect you from the cold. You come quietly, you understand? *Por Dios!* If you make a scene—if I am stopped or caused any trouble—then, beautiful as you are, I will kill you!"

He clung to her arm, hurrying her along. Her face and head were warm beneath the white hood. She could see very little. She was still weak and faint; confused, and with the horror of her father's death upon her.

All was a blur. She found that they were in the outer cave. She heard voices of the Antarcticans around their huts.

THERE WAS NO alarm. Several of Margones's band joined them surreptitiously.

"Are you ready, Margones?"

"Yes."

"We start now?"

"Yes, Vicente. Are the sleds waiting?"

Whispered words in Spanish. Helga could understand it.

"All in waiting, master. Who is this you have? The girl?"

"Get out of our way, idiot! Walk along with us quietly."

They were leaving the cavern; the cold outer air blew on Helga's face. Through the hood opening, she saw the stars of the deep purple night.

"Faster, Helga."

"Who is this, master—the girl?" Fingers plucked at her hood.

"Let her alone, damn you!" Margones rasped. "Vicente, it's gold! Millions of pesos of it! I got the location of it out of Johnson—he did know where it was, as we thought! Gold for us all. Hush! Here comes that ass, Umo."

Some of Naina's natives accosted them in the Antarctican tongue. Helga, helpless, stood tense with Margones clutching her. He evidently satisfied the natives. They passed on, along one of the streets of the settlement.

Several times Margones was accosted; always his grip tightened upon Helga as he stopped to answer.

They came at last to a lonely place at the edge of the village. She heard Margones giving directions to four of his men. They were to wait, hidden in the village, until Naina returned with the plane, and then seize it, and join Margones.

Sleds and dogs were here, in a bustle of activity. A loaded sled and three men started off; then another.

The bandits were quietly departing. Ten minutes or more passed, until at last there was only one sled left; and Helga found herself standing alone with Margones.

"Come, little sweet one, it is our turn to start now. The traveling will be easy over the trail they blaze for us. And in a few hours we will have the plane."

She stood in the starlight watching him as he moved about the sled with its line of harnessed dogs. The impulse to turn and run came to her. There were several huts here at the edge of the village, but they had been used by the bandits. They were unoccupied now. There seemed no one within immediate hearing; the dim settlement lights were several hundred yards away up the slope of the snow-field.

Margones was watchful. He came back to her. "You ride, Helga."

He put her on the sled, and enveloped her in furs. His touch lingered upon her warningly.

"Lie quiet."

The lead dog turned the sled at Margones's gesture. They started; slid out into the center of the packed, white roadway. The sled gathered speed. Margones ran at its handles, then he mounted it for a long swift descent.

14

HELGA AT BAY

HELGA GLANCED UP from the Primus stove over which she was bent. She asked, "Where did you get this, Margones?"

He grinned. "It came from one of your captured exploring expeditions. You've used this kind of stove before?"

"Yes."

She soon had the food ready. "Sit here, Margones."

It was their first camping place, a bowl-like depression in the snow-field with ice crags near by, and the deep purple dome of stars overhead. They had traveled fast for several hours, and had overtaken the bandit sleds which were in advance of them.

Margones kept Helga apart from his fellows. The bandits were encamped now a few hundred yards away, a noisy, roistering group. When they first arrived, Helga had heard considerable discussion concerning this American girl which Margones was taking with them. The news of the gold had spread among the bandits. They were jubilant; they did not want the complication of Helga. There had been one argument.

"You fool, don't you know we take extra danger having this American girl? Suppose a warplane comes?"

"You leave that to me."

"Lupe, the chief likes woman's beauty more than gold!"
A roar of laughter.

"You leave that to me. I am master here."

Helga sat listening. She heard them planning; they
had found at last what they were after. They were headed
now to verify the location of the gold; to find the nearest
hut where a radiophone would be available; to telephone
Santiago Pequeño. They would have a plane sent with the
national flag to record the strike for Chile.

There had been discussion also concerning Naina's plane;
they expected every moment that the four men they had
left in Naina's camp would arrive with it. During the trip
Margones had often cast a backward glance into the stars;
but so far there had been so sign of it.

Margones cursed the calmness of the weather. If a snowfall would only come and obliterate their trail—or if the
plane would come and take them aboard and thus leave
their tracks ending blindly here in the snow waste. But
the plane did not come. And the weather held calm and
cloudless.

Helga had fought and conquered her emotion. She was
pretending docility, even friendliness. She wondered if it
fooled this man.

Margones had been drunk when he entered Johnson's
cell. But he was sober enough afterward. He sat now by
the Primus stove with Helga. They ate the meal. She was
conscious always of his gaze upon her. He said abruptly:

"I know where this outcropping of gold is." He grinned.
"A Chilean city will be built there within a month. I and

my men will all be rich. You do not ask why I take you with me?"

It made her heart stop. She said, "No. Why?"

"Because you are a woman. I love you."

HE SAID IT with a sudden rush of intensity. He reached toward her, but she moved away.

She forced herself to say steadily, "You frighten me—because I am a woman."

"Frighten you?"

"Yes."

Their gazes met. He had flung back the white insulated garment which enveloped him. A gaudy sash was tied about his waist. A scarf was around his hair, exposed now as he pushed back his hood. His heavy blue-jowled face was smiling at her. A very modern, romantic fellow this Chilean renegade must have believed himself to be.

He said, *"Ay de mi!* I want not to frighten you, *chiquita."*

She wondered if he could see how really frightened she was. Her eyes held level; she added:

"Women of my race understand man's love. But fear does not mix with love. You do not want me afraid of you, Margones?"

He said, "My name is Ramón—"

She echoed, "Ramón." She even smiled at him, this murderer of her father. In her heart was a fierce hatred; but she smiled.

"No," he said. "You have nothing to fear from love—it brings joy, not fear. Am I not good to look at? Among all my people, it is said I am good to inspire woman's love—and your love I want!"

A vague confidence came to her. She said, "I feared you at first, but not so much now. No! Don't do that!"

His hand had gripped her shoulder; she shook it off vehemently. But she forced a smile. "You do not understand a woman like me, Ramón. A different race—love comes differently—slowly and only when fear is gone." She added, with a break in her voice against all her efforts to control it:

"You do not want the woman rebellious—the woman without love? That is—not interesting, is it, Ramón?"

"No," he said sullenly. From under his robe he brought the strip of fabric; and a small bottle. He was about to pour some of the perfume, but she checked him.

"No, Ramón. That is not the thing a man should do. You endanger us. We need all your great strength, your cleverness."

He hesitated. She reached for the little bottle.

"Try it," he said eagerly. "Smell the vapor from it. That is love, Helga."

"No. I was taking it from you. Let me keep it."

He took it back. But she had gained her point; he put it away.

For a time they ate in silence. Helga's gaze went over the scene around them.

It was an utter desolation, with this man and woman crouching by the flames of the tiny stove, and the bandits encamping near by. The sleds stood at hand. The dogs had been fed; they curled in the snow, tangling the harness. Off to the right a great ramp of snow slanted up obliquely. It loomed vaguely white in the starlit darkness.

Margones had said that after they rested, they would go that way. He had instruments; and he seemed familiar with the region—confident that he could find the mountain pass and the valley which Johnson had described to Helga.

Still the plane did not arrive from Naina's camp. Helga heard the bandits cursing it.

MARGONES SAID, "WELL, we go on with the sleds then, Helga. It is not so far now, this gold of ours."

"What will you do?" she asked.

"Do? We will locate it and camp by it. And then find a radiophone. In Santiago Pequeño they will be glad to know what we found. It will be for Chile, Helga—your country and mine. You will be a rich woman—richest of all in Santiago Pequeño. We will live there—or perhaps we go north, to Chile? Every luxury money brings will be yours, *niñita mía*—"

He would have touched her, but she avoided him again. "Not here, Ramón. Your men are watching."

He was flushed. "You like my plans? Great wealth— what woman can withstand it? And I am a man who knows what the woman wants—beautiful silks, and music, and the alcoholite of love."

Helga's gaze turned over the snow-waste to where their tracks went back toward Naina's camp. In the starlit darkness the trail could not be seen very far. Was any one following?

Would David, perhaps, be able to follow?

The bandits were ready to start again.

"Come, Helga."

"Yes," she said obediently.

They loaded the sled. Furtively Helga extracted a handkerchief from her pocket and dropped it in the snow.

"Yes, Ramón, I'm ready."

They started, all the sleds in a line now. Margones was jubilant. "Those fool men I left at the camp, they have failed to get the plane. But what matter. See, Helga, the snow comes."

The night was clouding over. A still calm fall of snow was beginning. It would not impede their traveling, but it would obliterate the trail.

They journeyed on, winding upward now into a broken country. Mountains showed ahead of them. Another hour. The snow was steadily falling.

The line of sleds wound at last into a mountain pass. Helga and Margones were now leading. Through the pass, into a little valley.

The golden mountain! The words echoed in Helga's mind, a requiem to her poor dead father. A cliff was here with a broad slope down from a ledge near its top—a ramp-like declivity down to the valley floor. Ice-crags were piled about; the snow lay thick. But there were places where the wind had bared the naked rock, with only the soft, present snowfall whitening it.

Margones stooped over a loose pile of stones. He held one up.

"Gold, Helga!"

She stared at the little chunk of rock, green-yellow with its gold. Nuggets of it here. This metallic rock, lying here hidden in the polar desolation—all the world's civilized luxury could be had in exchange for this! An avalanche of gold, fallen here at the foot of this cliff. There across the ragged, frozen mountain face, the outcropping vein lay like a swordslash. The "Johnson Lode," it is marked now on the charts.

The bandits gathered in triumph. They stood and gloated and picked up the stones and filled their pockets. The snowflakes swirled around them.

And Helga stood silent with the vision of her dead father's face before her. His words were echoing, "Our golden mountain."

The valley was open at the farther end—an upward slope toward the Chilean colony; Santiago Pequeño was that way, not over two hundred miles, Margones figured.

"We will camp here, Helga."

SOME OF THE bandits had mounted to the ledge up the cliff. There seemed to be a cave-mouth up there. The ascent was not too steep for the dogsleds.

The bandits called down.

"A cave," said Margones. "They have found a cave."

They climbed. The snow momentarily ceased. The stars briefly showed through a break in the clouds. The scene brightened.

"Helga, do you see that?"

Across the valley, a few miles away, was another jagged cliff-face. On its white, frozen side, a black spot showed. Margones studied it with his binoculars.

"A travelers' hut, Helga! Look— *Dios,* what luck is this!"

She took the glass. A little stone hut was perched on the rocks; the international flag, ragged and weather-worn, waved in the wind from the peak of its roof. Eerie little refuge, hanging at the edge of a cliff; set there so that storms might not bury it. An improvised stone staircase led down a hundred feet to the lower rock levels. Behind the hut, a white plateau stretched upward and back into a starry darkness.

"You see it, Helga?"

"Yes." She returned the binoculars. "Yes, I see it."

She sat at the entrance to the cave, watching them struggle up with their sleds and equipment. The snow was falling again; the stone hut across the valley was almost invisible in the murk.

"Lupe, come here; you will be the one to go."

Helga watched and listened while Margones and Lupe talked in Spanish. A small fellow, this Lupe Albeniz, swarthy and dark, with a fiercely overgrown black mustache. His white robe was hunched grotesquely at the waist with a broad black leather belt. An automatic hung there in a holster, a cylinder projector of the Johnson ray; and a long, broad knife, like an old-fashioned machete.

"Lupe, we will be busy here. You go send the radiophone. Call Marianao—*Señor* Auguste Marianao, Calle Valdez. You know him?"

"Yes—sure I do."

"Tell him that he will come in a plane. We have the gold located—it is the richest of what we could have hoped. Bring the Chilean flag, and official witnesses, so that at once we can notify London. Tell him that we will expect him in an hour or two. *Por Dios*, we're rich, Lupe! Tell him we will all of us be rich!"

The golden mountain!

Lupe, on foot presently started away. His white figure almost immediately was swallowed by the white falling snow.

Helga sat staring.

15

THE LIGHT IN THE HUT

"THEY STOPPED HERE."

"Yes, that's evident."

"I think, David, we're only an hour or two behind them—perhaps not even that much."

David and Naina had been traveling some six hours. The weather was still clear. David had feared every moment that it might snow and obliterate the trail. There was always that danger; the weather in Antarctica changed often with startling rapidity. It was as yet, a calm night of low temperature; but David, running at the handles of the sled, found himself warm.

Twice in the six hours they had stopped to rest and to eat. By the stars, David knew that they were heading in a general northerly direction across the floor of this great valley. The mountains of the encircling rim now loomed ahead of them, miles away as yet, a frowning wall against the sky. The Chilean colony lay this way, that was obvious.

It was arduous traveling, yet for the polar night in Antarctica the conditions were unusually favorable. A frozen tundra was this rocky floor, undulating like a great white desert. For miles it had been good sledging—drift snow fairly hard and firm. Then they had come to a broken

region. Frequent *bergschrunds*—gaping crevices of tremendous depths formed as the body of a glacier moves from
the snowfield—were encountered. The bandits' trail picked
its way past them.

They crossed what to David seemed some frozen, land-
locked sea, then again came upon a glacier with walls of
rock from a mountain spur. A field of *sérac* ice was here,
wedged masses of icy pinnacles created by the dragging
strains on the glacier surface.

They made at times no more than a few miles an hour;
but David knew that Margones could do no better, if as
well. He thought of Helga, out here in this cold purple
night. A sled so easily could side-slip. He prayed that they
might not overtake Margones's sled with tragedy come
upon it.

The rough area was passed; they came again upon the
frozen plains.

"He stopped here," said Naina. They stood beside the
evidence of where the bandits had made a brief camp—
the remains of food; a melted, refrozen place in the snow
where some sort of stove had been set.

"An hour or two ahead of us," Naina repeated.

David, poking about the remains of the camp, stooped
suddenly.

"What is that?" she demanded sharply.

David held it up. Helga's handkerchief.

"She thinks we may be following." He made no further
comment. In the dimness of the night, especially in broken
country, they could approach fairly close to the bandits
without discovery. But not too close.

"We had better rest awhile, Naina. And the dogs need it."

He fed the dogs, and then got out a sleeping-bag. "Don't you want to sleep for an hour or two?"

"No," she said.

They sat together and ate some dried, salted meat and fish. They heated water.

WHENEVER THEY STOPPED like this, to David came the consciousness of how alone they were. The barrier between them was so frail a thing. He found now that her gaze was steadily on him. As always, it set his heart wildly pounding.

"Naina!"

He laid a hand on her shoulder. The impulse came to sweep her in his arms. He had so often felt it! He repeated her name unsteadily.

This barrier between them—if he could once hold her in his arms, his lips on hers, it would break down.

He thought wildly, "She doesn't know what love means—but she can feel it, feel what I am feeling."

"Naina, dear."

He abruptly held her in his arms. His face went to hers. But he saw fear in her eyes. Fear of this torrent sweeping her.

She pushed at him. "David! Why—" The fear turned to anger. "Let me go!"

It was exasperating. "You foolish little girl, don't—fight with me—"

"Let me go!"

Anger. It was her instinctive defense. He saw that beneath the show of anger, she was really frightened.

He released her. "I'm sorry, Naina."

Some one was inside the hut!

There was a silence. He watched her anger fading. She said presently: "We mustn't stay here too long. Would he dare take Helga over the Chilean border?"

They discussed it as though nothing had happened between them. Naina was convinced that the bandit was in love with Helga, desiring her so that he had forced all his men to this sudden flight, and that he was taking Helga over the Chilean border, where in Santiago Pequeño he might force her to marry him.

"The United States would not bother him then, David."

As an explanation of Margones's purpose it did not sound very plausible to David. But he could think of nothing better.

He said now, cautiously: "Do you suppose there's a raidophone near?"

She knew of one. She thought it was some thirty miles ahead.

"If they head that way," she said. "But why, David?"

"I was thinking it might be difficult for us to attack Margones. He has twenty men or more, armed."

Her eyes were wide. "Use weapons against me? They would not dare."

"They might. They're desperate." He saw her annoyance rising, but he plunged. "They used weapons and attacked your plane. I was thinking—are you friendly toward Chile? The government, I mean?"

"No. They have never recognized me as anything but the daughter of the White Bandit. My Antarctican government—"

"Well, I thought we might phone somewhere for help, for a plane."

"The Norwegians," she said. "There is the Whaling Company at Alert Bay. I have nothing against them."

"Yes, if we phoned, a plane could reach us in a few hours. Is it a thousand miles to Alert Bay? Not over that."

It was farthest from David's plans. But now he only wanted to get Naina to locate this phone-hut. He gazed at the stars; a sheen of mist was over them.

"We'd better get started," he said. "If the snow comes and obliterates the trail—we're finished—"

A blizzard, striking them out here, might be more than they could weather. But neither of them was considering that.

THEY STARTED AGAIN, and traveled another hour or two. The snowfall came; thick white flakes were now falling steadily, but still there was very little wind.

They struggled forward, lashing the dogs to top speed. They were winding into the white foothills of mountains. The bandits' trail was filling up. David saw it with sinking heart.

They passed into a white gorge. Steeply up through drift snow. A wind was here. Whirlies danced around them—whirlpools of the drift snow, caught and tossed by the wind, ghostly dervishes whirling in the dimness. They struggled on, just as, not much more than an hour ahead of them now, the bandits with Helga, had struggled.

They came out of the gorge into a broad valley. The wind eased up. The snow had suddenly ceased a few moments before; but now it came again. The valley was a dull gray-white blur. The bandits' trail, almost hidden now, led off to the left.

Naina said suddenly: "I think I've passed over this valley in the plane. The phone-hut is off there." She gestured to the right. She told David what she remembered of the topography of this valley.

David said, "There's a storm coming."

It seemed so; a premonitory blast of wind, flinging the drift against them so that the dogs stopped and huddled with their drooping backs to it. A blast suddenly ended and gone. But David knew it would come again.

"Well, if you say there are cavemouths over there, Naina," he gestured the way Margones had taken, "he'll camp here. He won't dare go any farther in this. We'd better get to the travelers' hut if we can find it."

She acquiesced. They left the trail and started off to the right. At that moment Margones and his band were camping on the ledge a few miles away in the other direction.

The snow every moment came thicker. There was another blast. They weathered it, and struggled on.

Naina was not sure enough of the locality. They went up a broken frozen slope; they reached the open uplands of a plateau.

"We're going wrong," said Naina.

They turned and went diagonally back. To David came the fear that they were lost. And unmistakably this was the start of a bad storm.

They saw the little stone hut like a haven in the murk close ahead of them. The snow was blowing around it. The international flag at its peak was a tiny waving spot. They were on the upper level, behind the hut. David saw that it stood on a brink, fronting the storm-tossed valley.

They dashed forward. But something made David bring them to a sudden halt. The sled stopped; the dogs turned their backs to the wind. It had seemed to David that a moving spot of light had showed at the hut. It was only a few hundred feet ahead now, a dark oblong in the gloom of the night.

Was some one there? It seemed so.

David commanded the lead dog to lie down. He shoved Naina behind him.

"I'll go on foot."

They crept forward, dim, cautious white figures. David gripped his automatic. The little building loomed ahead of them. Its windows were barred with shutters. The spot of light was gone now. The place seemed deserted.

But was it?

They crouched at a corner of the building. The wind drove the snow about them with a low whine. A window was near at hand. Through its shutter-slits a blue flare of light was flickering!

Tiny flashes of blue light. Some one was here! Some one, inside the hut, using a radiophone!

"Naina, wait—keep away!"

With his ear to the shutters, David could hear. And he found Naina pressing against him, listening also.

A man was inside, talking in Spanish, his voice mingled with the hissing and flickering of the instrument. David caught a little of it, and Naina whispered a translation. One of Margones's men talking to Santiago Pequeño. Gold discovered here! The radiophone was equipped with the code-wave apparatus—the bandit could talk freely. Gold had been discovered here years ago by Johnson, of the old Blakely expedition, he said, but never recorded. Margones could get it now with the Chilean flag—

For a moment David was stricken into inactivity. A Chilean plane would be coming within an hour or so.

Within the hut, the bandit disconnected the instrument. David found his wits.

"You wait here," he whispered. "I'll go around the front—the door may be open."

On the brink of the cliff he crept along the front wall of the hut. He saw that the narrow door stood open.

16

IN THE STORM SHELTER

THERE WAS ONLY one man in the room—a small, swarthy fellow in a white garment with a belt around his middle. He stood by the radiophone which he had just disconnected. The room was almost dark, only the vague sheen of light from the fading instrument tubes. David crouched in the doorway. The bandit was fumbling about.

The light faded into blank darkness. David felt Naina beside him.

"Get back," he whispered vehemently.

The room was suddenly flooded with a dull-yellow vacuum glare; the bandit had found the switch. It startled David; he stood revealed by the light. The bandit saw him. His lower jaw dropped; his fiercely upturned mustache twitched with his surprise.

David's weapon was raised. "Put up your hands!"

But the fellow, with disconcerting promptness, took a header and flung himself on the floor. David's shot went over his head. The report split the little room with a muffled, echoing crack. David followed it with a leap. He landed upon the half crouching figure; he felt his sleeve rip with an upflung knife thrust.

They rolled on the stone floor David was far the stronger, and more than fifty pounds heavier. He caught the fellow's wrist, twisted the knife away. David had dropped his automatic; he saw Naina dash forward and pick it up.

"Get back, Naina, I've got him!"

The bandit was squirming, with David sitting on his chest. The Chilean tried to get his automatic from the holster at his belt; but David reached for it, jerked it out and flung it back to Naina. And from his adversary's belt David also ripped the cylinder-weapon of the Johnson ray.

The little fellow suddenly squealed, "I stop! I stop!"

He twisted violently, trying to throw David off; and David cuffed him in the face.

"No, *señor*—I stop!"

"Well, if you stop, lie still, you damn fool."

He lay quiet. David pulled him to his feet. The Chilean stood eying them, then quailed as he saw Naina.

"Got any other weapons?" David demanded.

"No, *señor*—*no tengo ningunos.*"

David searched him. "What's your name?"

"He's Lupe Albeniz," Naina burst out. She flung a flood of Spanish at him, and he cringed before her. He was obviously far more frightened of Naina than of David.

"Easy, Naina." David pushed her away. His mind was flying. Gold discovered here. Helga's gold! United States gold! The Chileans were coming to claim it. The message had gone in; too late to stop it now.

"How far is Margones from here?" David demanded.

"*Señor?*"

"I said—Naina, does he understand English or doesn't he?"

Lupe evidently wanted to be ingratiating. His face was gray; his dark eyes swam with fear of Naina.

"Me understan' the English—not so fast, you spik."

"Ask him, Naina."

HE LISTENED TO their Spanish. Outside the little stone room the wind was now howling. Snow was blowing through the open doorway. David slid the door closed.

"Watch him, Naina! What's he say?"

"A few miles from here; not far, across the valley. You could see their camp from here if the snow would stop."

Lupe described it. He might be lying, but he seemed truthful.

"Is Helga there?"

"*Sí, señor.*" He added with a grin: "She love Ramón—they get the married in Santiago Pequeño."

"Shut up," said David. He cast his eye about the room. It was some thirty feet long by half as wide. There was the phone mechanism; the lights; a storage electrical heater; an electrical stove; a few pieces of dilapidated furniture; a litter of bedding; two built-in bunks.

Across one end, a partition divided off a smaller space into another—a windowless room. Tinned food stood here on a shelf; there were ropes; a block and tackle; coils of wire; spare radio tubes and vacuum light tubes; and a box of tools. Also some cooking utensils.

David seized a length of rope and came back.

"Stand away, Naina."

Lupe eyed him. "What you do?"

"Shut up. I won't hurt you."

"She no hurt me?"

"No," David assured him. "I'm going to tie you up, that's all."

"You sen' me Santiago Pequeño—*no he hecho nada*—" He wandered into swift Spanish apologies and excuses.

"Never mind that," said David. He roped the little bandit securely and carried him bodily into the storeroom.

"You lie there. Not a word out of you. Understand?"

"*Sí, señor.* I no spik, *nada.*"

"Good." David came back and faced Naina.

"What you going to do?" she demanded.

"Phone for help. We haven't any time to lose. You found the heat switch?"

"Yes."

The room was warming. Naina had closed the glassite windows; the electrical stove was glowing.

"Good enough. We'll have to stay here for awhile. Listen to that storm."

It surged about the compact little building. David flung off his furs. He stood gazing down at Naina.

"Take off that cloak; you'll be too hot." He helped her discard it. He did it swiftly; he was in a hurry, but he did not want to show it. Something in Naina's watchful gaze warned him.

"There's food in there," he said, "and utensils. How about fixing us something hot?"

He turned away, but she seized him. "Where are you going to phone—phone to whom?"

"Little America," he said shortly.

"No! I won't let you!" She gripped him. "I won't let you!"

HE FINALLY PUSHED her away. Too much time had passed already. Little America was much farther away than Santiago Pequeño, and the Chileans were already warned and preparing to come.

"Naina, don't be a fool."

"I won't let you!"

She stood in her long white dress; her pale golden braids dangled; her eyes were blazing.

Strange, imperious beauty!

She reached to seize one of the automatics which she had placed on a chair along with the cylinders of the Johnson cold light. But David stopped her.

"Don't bother me, Naina. I'm in a hurry, can't you see it?"

Their challenging gazes crossed. And as she stood fronting him with breast swiftly rising and falling, abruptly David's annoyance was gone. A wild tumult swept him.

"Naina, you don't understand."

"I won't let you call the Americans."

He murmured as though to himself, "I'll make you understand."

His arms went around her. He crushed her against him.

"Let me go! David—let me go!"

She fought, struggled, like a child against his huge lean body. She pounded at his chest with her fists.

"Let me go!"

"No, not this time."

He was bending her backward. As she fought, his senses swept off upon a torrent of passion.

"Naina—I love you! Don't you know it?"

He held her face, against all her twisting efforts. Her lips were parted with trembling breath.

"David—please!"

Fear was in her eyes. But something else now; a coming tenderness. Surrender.

"Naina, I love you."

As he kissed her, and she helplessly fought, he felt her suddenly go limp in his arms.

"Naina, this is love! Don't you understand?" He kissed her again.

Limp in his arms, now she hid her face against his shoulder. He kissed her hair; and as her white arms came up, and her fingers gripped his shoulder, he kissed her hand.

"Love, Naina—and it makes everything different. You haven't understood."

"David, I—"

"Say it!"

"I—"

"Say it!"

She murmured, "I—love you, David."

"Love me?" His passion melted into sudden tenderness. "Love me? You know it now! Kiss me, Naina. Look! I've let you go. I'm not holding you."

He stood drooping, with his arms at his sides. And she flung herself upon him, clinging with her arms about his neck, her eager lips held up to him, and drew his face down, and kissed him.

"There—does that prove I love you? Does it, David? And this—and this. Oh, David, I never knew that love could be a thing like this!"

17

THE DECOY

NAINA SAT WATCHING David as he connected the radio-phone.

"Can you get them?"

"Yes, I hope so."

He smiled into her luminous eyes. "We'll do our best. If only this storm doesn't hold them back!"

He made the connections. There was no answer to the call, for ten minutes or more. The wind howled outside the hut.

"Oh, David. Helga's over there—they'll take her to Santiago Pequeño. How can we get her back? He can force her to say she married him voluntarily. The United States would have no claim on her then."

The call was answered. Little America came in.

"I want Joseph Welch," David said briefly. "David Dragon speaking. International hut eleven." The number was on the instrument. "Is he there?"

"Yes, I can find him," said the operator's voice.

"Hurry with it! Danger here—matter of life and death! I want the United States wave code—don't want this picked up anywhere else."

After what seemed an eternity to David, I came on the circuit. He told me hurriedly what had transpired.

"A plane available there, Joe?"

There was. The warplanes from Dunedin had not yet arrived. We had done nothing during those hours since Naina's threat, except try to communicate with her and wait for the warplanes. But we had a commercial plane available.

My heart sank at what David was telling me. Helga, captured by the Chilean bandits!

"Just where are you, David?"

"International Station Eleven."

"Where is that?"

"How do I know where it is? Look it up on your registry chart."

I could do that of course. "We'll start at once."

"Yes. Bring official witnesses and the flag. And men and weapons, Joe; there are twenty of these bandits."

He outlined his plan. I was to fly directly to the hut. We would have to figure some way to rescue Helga. To attack the bandits openly might mean her death.

"Hurry, Joe. If the Chileans get there first—I'm helpless here—they'll plant the Chilean flag, record the strike officially and be gone with Helga."

"Yes. I'll rush."

"How's the weather, Joe?"

"Terrible."

The storm was raging in Little America even worse than in David's locality. But it would be a flight with the wind.

"All the better," said David hurriedly. "The Chilean plane will be heading into it. Do your best, Joe."

He presently disconnected.

"Nothing we can do but wait, Naina."

HE ENVISAGED THE two planes—one from the Chilean Colony and one from Little America—racing here on the wings of the storm; each eager to be the first to plant their national flag, to record this golden mountain, to establish a new settlement here.

But it was more than that. If the Chileans came first, Helga would be snatched away. And if the plane from Little America came first—David shuddered as he thought of Helga, over there with Margones.

How could the bandits be openly attacked? Margones, with his golden prize snatched from him, his own safety menaced, would undoubtedly kill Helga at once.

"Nothing to do, but wait." He met Naina's queerly earnest face. Gentle now, tender, her eyes luminous as stars.

"I was thinking, David."

She drew him to the door and they opened it. The wind and snow swirled in, a frigid blast—they flung the door closed.

David had seen that although the wind was every moment stronger, it was, for the moment, hardly snowing at all.

Naina clung to him. "I was thinking—won't Margones wonder why Lupe doesn't come back? Do you suppose he'll send over here to see what's happened?"

They had been in the hut now perhaps half an hour or more. Such a possibility had not occurred to David, but it was obvious.

The door had an interior lock. They turned it, and flung down into place a heavy bar. The windows were all barred;

these international huts were constructed to give refuge from possible attack.

They went to one of the windows fronting the valley, slid its shutter aside. Through the double glassite panes the murk of the night was visible. Blackness overhead; scudding black clouds; wind-clouds, rather than snow. Momentarily a patch of stars showed.

"You suppose our light might be seen by Margones, David?"

"I don't know. Perhaps."

It seemed to David that he could vaguely make out the form of the mountains across the valley floor. But no light showed over there. Would Margones come, or send others of his men to investigate what had happened to Lupe?

The captive was lying quietly in the storeroom. There had not been a word, or a sound out of him.

"I was thinking, David—you said, nothing to do, but wait; is that all we can do? Do we dare wait? I was thinking—my father once told me about the Alpha International Helio Code. Do you know it?"

He did; and comprehension came to him, of a possible chance.

"Does Helga know it?" she asked.

"Yes," he said. His mind flung back to a time when he had discussed it with Helga.

"Do you suppose, David, that Margones knows it? If he does not—and Helga could see and read our flashes—"

They went in to Lupe. Naina asked him in Spanish, "Did you ever hear of the Alpha International Helio Code?"

"Sure I did, *señorita*," he responded eagerly.

"Does Margones understand it?"

"No," he said scornfully. "No one over there understand it but me; I can work it. What you—"

Naina demanded, "Does Margones know that you understand the code? Did you ever tell him so?"

"Sure, *señorita*."

"Think well, Lupe. If you're lying, I'll find it out. You know how I punish."

"I speak truth, *señorita*. Margones, he has seen me use a helio."

THEY LEFT HIM. "You think he's lying, Naina?"

She did not. Lupe was the most skilled with transmission instruments of any of Margones's men, which was why the bandit leader had sent him to the radiophone, here in the hut.

They decided to chance it. Naina took the cylinder of the Johnson ray. It was the strongest light they had.

"From the doorway, David—don't dare use it in here."

They put on their outer robes, and stood in the doorway, with the room dark behind them. The wind plucked and tore at them. There was another patch of stars overhead; the brink of the cliff with its ladderlike steps was close to the doorway.

The valley stretched before them, a dim gray void with its conformations almost visible. Across it, up against the sullen clouds and the patch of stars, outlines of the opposite mountain crags vaguely showed.

David stood with the cylinder which Naina had shown him how to operate. He sent a flash—a blue-white stab of light into the murk.

Then another. Another. Long and short. Calling, in the Alpha code:

"Helga. Helga."

Blue stabs of light. Even out here in the frigid polar night, the cold of the Johnson ray flung up a white mist. The wind tore it away. The blue light stabbed steadily into the darkness:

"Helga. Helga."

Would she see it? Would she be able to answer? Or was Lupe lying? Would Margones answer? If so, then David would have betrayed himself. But if not, then Margones would think Lupe was calling, and he would get Helga to translate it for him.

David waited. Then he tried it again.

"It isn't visible over there, Naina."

She clung to him as a blast of the wind flung a swirl of drift-snow over them. They huddled, protecting their faces with the hoods.

"Try it again." She almost had to shout to make him hear her.

"Helga."

They saw in the distant darkness a flash of blue seeming to answer them.

18

SPRINGING THE TRAP

THE BANDITS WERE dispersed about the small cave, with its single narrow entrance. With this shelter from the wind, it was warmer in here; the heat from the several small stoves was soon apparent.

Helga sat apart. No one seemed bothering with her. In the babble of Spanish she was neglected. But not wholly forgotten. She moved once toward the tunnel; Margones immediately came forward.

"Go back, Helga. Sit still. Soon we have the food ready."

He rejoined his fellows. Helga listened to their triumphant talk. The four men they had left at Naina's camp had evidently failed to steal her plane. Perhaps they had been discovered and killed. What of it? Four less with whom to divide this gold. The plane from Santiago Pequeño would be here soon. Lupe was experienced with the radiophone— he would have sent the message by now.

Time passed. They began to wonder why Lupe did not return. He had trouble making the radiophone work, perhaps? Well, Lupe was skillful with instruments.

Margones brought food to Helga, and sat with her while they ate it. The wind howled outside the cave. Inside, the fumes of alcoholite were heavy. The bandits were in gay mood. The talk rose higher. Helga heard a lewd remark from a near-by group. Suddenly half a dozen flushed evil faces were staring at her.

"—this Yankee girl—they say Yankee girls are—"

Margones whispered, "I will stay by you, little sweet one—"

He was grinning; but she saw his fingers go to his automatic. Margones was sober. He had kept away from the alcoholite this time; he had cautioned his men, but they would not heed him.

Helga said, "There's so little fresh air in this cave, Ramón—this perfume—"

Margones touched her. "Niñita—think when we are alone, to breathe it freely."

"Yes, Ramón. But—but now, I'm frightened."

He rose to his feet. "Come, *chica*—of them all, only you and I have sense. We will sit nearer the outside."

A guard was at the cave-mouth. He was annoyed at having to be there away from the fun.

"Well then, go inside," said Margones. "I will wait here. Soon Lupe will return."

A patch of stars showed overhead. The white snow-covered valley was faintly illumined. It was snowing fitfully; the wind howled, then suddenly was still. Then howled again.

"Lupe will—"

Margones stood staring. "What is that? You see it, Helga?"

A blue stab of light through the murk across the valley. Faint, faraway blue flashes, coming evidently from the little hut over there.

Crouching in the snow, huddled in their white garments, Helga and Margones gazed fascinated. Flashes of tiny blue lightnings. The Johnson ray. Lupe's ray, obviously.

To Margones the signal meant nothing intelligible. But Helga stared with pounding heart. Uneven, waning stabs of light, like a helio beam.

She read to herself: "H—" The Alpha code! She read: *"Helga. Helga."*

"That is Lupe," said Margones. "What, by the devil, can he want?"

Margones was puzzled; it seemed to Helga that there was chagrin in his tone. Chagrin because he could not read the signals, and was ashamed to admit it before this girl? She thought, of course, that it was Lupe signalling.

"Helga. Helga."

WHY DID HE call "Helga?" Why not call "Margones?" Something within the girl told her to be cautious.

"That looks like the Alpha Code, Ramón. Does Lupe know it?"

"Yes. Is that what it is?"

"I think so. Can't you read it?"

The bandit had too much at stake; he overcame his pride. "No. Can you?"

"Wait," she said. "I think so." Something, some instinct, was warning her to go slow. She said, "Let me have your cylinder; I'll answer him—"

She stood with Margones steadying her. She flashed: *"Lupe."*

And then her heart leaped and began wildly thumping. From across the storm-tossed night came the helioed words:

"This is David, are you Helga?"

"Yes."

She turned to Margones. She caught her breath, but she said steadily:

"It is Lupe, calling to you, Ramón."

"What does he say? By the Virgin, if he has not sent that message—ask him."

She sent: *"I am Helga. Tell me what to do."*

A long answer. She said: "Lupe had trouble with the phone. But he got them. He told them in Santiago Pequeño to land the plane at the hut."

Margones cursed. *"Por Dios!* Why?"

Helga was quick-witted. Resourceful. She was outwardly calm, for all her thumping heart. She said:

"He has a plan, Ramón. It is a good one; wait, listen."

She was constructing her words partly by what David helioed from the hut, and partly by conditions as she knew them to be here at the cave. She was aware now that Lupe had been captured by David and Naina, and that David wanted her to trick Margones into bringing her across the valley.

"Ramón, listen: he says for you and me to come over. It is not far. He says, why should we divide our royalty on the gold with all your men? He has a plan to avoid that."

"What plan?" Margones was interested; greed was in his voice. *"Sangre de Dios,* a bold fellow, this Lupe! But why not? Listen to those *borrachones* in there!"

From the cave came shouts and drunken laughter. Helga departed from David's instructions with details of her own.

"Ramón, I don't want to stay here. I'm afraid of them." She put all the allurement she could muster into her pleading voice. "Ramón, why should we divide our gold? With Lupe, because we must, but that's enough. We've got to take into shares some of the men coming in the plane. And, Ramón—over there in the hut it will be warm. You and I alone—and Lupe is very discreet."

He clutched at her. "Helga, *niñita mía*—"

"THEY'RE COMING, NAINA! See them!"

From the window shutters they could see the quavering light down in the valley. A moving hand-flash light beam, dimly yellow, lost in the swirling snow. It bobbed into view again, like a tiny boat on a storm-tossed sea, but it came steadily forward; and presently David and Naina saw the two white figures struggling on foot through the drifts.

"Get Lupe out! Threaten him."

"Yes," she agreed.

The snow-covered figures of Helga and Margones came mounting the ladder-stairs up the cliff; Helga was in front with the bandit holding her.

"Ready, Naina?"

David cuffed the released Lupe. "There—that's a sample! Understand me?"

"Oh, *sí, señor.*"

"And I'll shoot—you'd drop like a rat before you knew what's happened to you."

They pushed him to the door; they crouched out of sight behind him, with automatics leveled.

Naina murmured in Spanish, "You call out, Lupe—then you step backward."

"Yes, I understand. I obey."

They heard Margones's voice:

"*Hola!* Lupe! Lupe!"

David opened the door, keeping behind it. Lupe stood there in the light, with an effort to hide his fright, and called his greeting: "Ramón! Come in. *Entra Vd.*" Lupe stepped back.

Helga came first over the threshold. She saw David and Naina, with Lupe quivering to one side.

"Hello, Lupe!" She turned back. "Warm in here, Ramón. Come."

Margones entered.

David leaped on him and bore him down.

19

ON THE MOUNTAIN CREST

THEY ROPED MARGONES and Lupe and laid them side by side in the storeroom. Naina stood over Margones.

"You dared to disobey me?" The old imperious ring was in her voice.

David drew her away. "No, Naina."

"But you have not hurt him—not punished him."

He smiled gently. "He will be punished. In Little America he will stand trial for murder." He put an arm over her shoulders. "You don't have to worry your little head about it—you're not judge and jury and executioner any more, Naina."

Helga stood gazing at them; at Naina's flush—and her obedience to David.

"Naina, you're beautiful," she said. They faced each other in the main room. "Beautiful, and so different."

"Am I? You're beautiful, too, Helga."

Without the outer white robe, Helga stood trim and competent-looking in her military cape of blue and red.

"Am I? You like this?"

David exploded, "Good Heavens, at a time like this!"

David had already hinted to Helga the reason for Naina's change. The girls clung to each other.

"Joe could get here in an hour," said David. "Look here—we've got to plan something."

David was afraid that any moment now the Chilean plane might come. It seemed incredible that it could buck this wind, roaring as it must be in the higher altitude. But still it might get through. If so, it was due here now.

"We've got to plan something, do something. With Margones's men over there, holding the claim, the Chileans can plant their flag and it will all be perfectly legal. I think I'll try calling Little America again to see when Joe left, and what the weather is."

Helga said, "Do that. Come over here, Naina, I want to talk to you." They sat apart, while David hurriedly connected the instrument.

"Love him, Naina?"

"Oh, Helga!"

"Well, Joe could make me feel like that, only he doesn't know it. But this is no time to talk of love. I've an idea."

She told Naina how the bandits were roistering in the cave. "I had it figured out for Margones. Before we left them awhile ago, Margones told his men to go ahead and get drunk. Well, with him out of the way, they would anyhow. They're all drunk over there now." She added irrelevantly, "They put some queer equipment in these international huts sometimes. Have you looked around the storeroom, Naina?"

"No. Why?"

"I was thinking, if I could find a package of pins, and a pair of shears—"

Naina stared at her.

"And I'm sure there'll be tacks or nails, and a hammer. Come on, let's look."

David got Little America. The plane had started shortly after his previous call. The weather was about the same.

"What are you doing?" he demanded of the girls.

They had found what they were after. They were both trembling with excitement. They told him the plan. He listened, amazed; but it was feasible. The bandits, a score in number, would be roistering in the cave. Only one entrance, Helga was sure of that. They would all be stupefied by the alcoholite—there would doubtless be no guard.

DAVID AND THE girls had automatics, and three of the Johnson cylinders—Naina's, the one belonging to Lupe, and one they had just taken from Margones.

"It can be done!" David exclaimed. "We'll try it."

Within fifteen minutes they were ready. They verified that Margones and Lupe could not escape.

"Better gag them," said Helga. "No use having them shout."

They shrouded themselves in their outer garments. They took the handflash Margones had brought.

Helga carried a package and a coil of rope. David took the rope.

Helga said, "I'll put this other under my cloak. You think it's large enough, David?"

"Of course. What matter?"

Naina said, "Give it to me, please; I want to carry it."

With a last look around they started. They extinguished all the lights of the hut, and closed its door. David had again called Little America. The operator there was still in communication with the oncoming American plane.

David sent word that the plane was not to land by the hut, but across the valley at the gold claim.

They went down the ladder steps—endlessly, it seemed, down into the torrent of whirling drift snow. They struggled out across the valley. The floor was a smother of tossing drifts. Whirlies sucked around them, dancing, ghostly unreal. Or again, a blast of shriveled, frozen flakes enveloped them like a sand-storm—a stinging blast that could not be faced; under it they wilted and crouched until it had eased off.

Helga was more familiar with the conformation of the valley than were the others. She led the way, with David and Naina behind her. There was no snow falling from the clouds now. Those were still angry black masses up there, but they were thin and split by the wind. Like flying scud they lay strewn across the star field.

In David's judgment, the worst of the storm was over. The wind presently would die. It must have been fearful in the open air above the mountains. Down here in the inclosed valley it was freakish, but without its power now.

The valley was brightening a trifle. The starlight was breaking through, and the line of mountains ahead was dimly visible; the peaked razorback mound which was Johnson's claim strike—Helga pointed it out; a sharply ascending slope up to a ledge; the cave mouth there where the roistering bandits were encamped; a ramp of frozen surface to its left, sloping to jagged pinnacle of the upper crest.

It was all dim and vague. From the cave-mouth itself the bandits could hardly have seen the figures floundering through the drifts on the valley floor, even had any of

Margones's men been interested enough or sober enough to look. But David took no chances. They used no hand light; and they bore steadily off to the left.

An hour, it seemed to David—but it could not have been nearly that long. He feared every moment, with this slackening wind, that the Chilean plane might appear. But the stars off there showed nothing. Perhaps, heading into the violence of that wind, the Chileans had been forced down. That would account for the delay. Then the official expedition would come on by land. The valley off there opened up a slope to the higher distant plateau. The Chilean sleds would come racing down it, glaring with headlights and with flags flying.

DAVID'S THOUGHTS WERE sharply brought back to realities. Helga twitched at the fur of his sleeve. She gestured toward the bottom of the ramp.

"I think we should go this way."

They began the climb. Another ten minutes and they reached the level of the ledge—a few hundred feet from the cave mouth.

Silent, frozen darkness. They thought they heard a distant, muffled laugh.

"On up," said David, softly. It was dark here against this mountain; but the valley now was brighter than ever before. The wind had almost died; stars showed in several broad patches overhead. The white scene was beginning to glow serene under the starlight. Had the American plane fallen? It too could arrive any time now—if it had not fallen.

There was no sign of anything out there save purple-white, frozen, desolate emptiness.

They climbed for the crest. They stood upon it at last,

fifty feet above the cave level, and a hundred and fifty above the valley floor. A wan shimmer was up here—white drifts, with the starlight on them. Pinnacles of rock upstanding like spires.

David uncoiled the rope. "We're in time!"

"Yes." The girls stood with him. Naina added, "There isn't any chance that if Margones's men came out on the ledge they could see us?"

"No," said Helga.

The ledge was hidden beneath the overhanging brow of this upper region.

"Besides," said Helga contemptuously, "they're all too drunk on alcoholite to do anything."

The cave-mouth was close enough so that in the silence now, with the wind no more than a gentle breeze, the sounds of the merrymaking bandits floated up.

David coiled the rope. He flung an end of it, which on his second trial went over a rock spire above them. He picked up the fallen end and pulled the rope taut.

"Now!" said Naina.

Helga exclaimed, "Look there!"

Across the wan starry valley, on the plateau in the direction of Santiago Pequeño, lights showed. A line of lights, coming up over an undulation of the snowfield. Lights, blazing on a line of speeding dog sleds. The mining claim officials from the Chilean colony!

The line came over the crest and began the coasting descent; sleds, black blobs against the snow pack, white in the glare of the lights they bore—and resplendent with their national banners waving in the wind.

20

"I AM AN AMERICAN"

ONE SCENE MORE. I picture it as I personally saw it. Our expedition in the large commercial triplane from Little America was ready within half an hour after I got David's radiophone from the hut in the distant mountains. We took four sleds and their necessary dogs in the event that our plane went down and the journey had to be continued over the snow. It seemed a likely possibility.

We did our best to hasten the departure. I gathered the willing official witnesses. They would gladly have made the flight gratis, but the legal award of a small share in the royalties from the strike was an extra inducement.

The news of what we were doing spread rapidly throughout the town. Little America was excited. A crowd of furred figures stood in the storm at the flying field to see us off. We rose with flags flying; a spotlight from the field clung to us as we winged away.

I need not detail the flight. There were forty of us on board. We maintained for some time our communication with the Little America operator. We got the relay of David's second message—not to land at the hut, but to fly across the little valley. It told us the topography of the region. We made a sketch map of it.

I recall that it occurred to me to wonder that this gold could lie so close to Hut Eleven and not have been discovered when the hut was built. Yet there have been several such precedents in Antarctica. The valley, and all that cliffside, might easily have been buried deep in snow that season when the international officials were there.

At all events, after all these years the Johnson Lode was waiting, virgin territory unclaimed—waiting for the raising of the first flag. And it would not be a Chilean flag if we on this plane could prevent it.

We flew almost directly with the wind. Then we lost connection with Little America. We had tried several times to pick up Hut Eleven, but could not.

It seemed an interminable flight. I became obsessed with the idea that the Chileans would be there first. They had the storm against them, but they had less than half as far to go—and they had doubtless started first.

All this was overshadowed by my fear for Helga. All that I had heard was that she was in the hands of Margones's bandits.

The wind gradually lost its force; the stars came out in patches. Flying low, we skimmed over the Antarctic frozen uplands. Grimly forbidding wastes lay down there in the starlight. It seemed, as I gloomily stared down at the desolation sliding under me, incredible that anything could exist here worth man's struggle. Incredible that through the centuries this frozen continent was here, unassailed by man—and now to be the arena of nations competing for its riches.

We came at last over the rim of the valley, unmistakably our goal. In the observation cabin, where I was seated, a chorus of exclamations burst from the men around me. But I sat tense, staring downward.

LIKE A STAGE setting, viewed with futuristic modernity from the air above, the climax of the drama in the valley was revealed. White-smothered valley floor, pale in the starlight. At one side the tiny blob which was the dark travelers' hut. On the other side, Johnson's razorback mountain ridge; a ledge and a cave mouth. A group of Margones's bandits had evidently just come to the cave mouth from inside. They stood, befuddled with alcoholite, staring at the valley.

The Chilean expedition was just arriving! The last of its sleds was hauling up into a group at the bottom of the upward slope. A glare of the expedition lights. Officials tumbling from the sleds.

The man beside me shoved binoculars into my hand. "Look up on top, Welch!"

On the crest of the mountain over the cave three figures were standing. Suddenly the spotlight from our descending plane fell upon them, revealing them brightly.

I raised the binoculars. David, with Naina and Helga, stood there among the frozen crags. A rope had been caught upon an upper spire. David held the lower end of the rope.

And up there on the rope a little flag was flying! Waving triumphantly in the wind; vivid, resplendent in the white searchlight glare. Claiming this golden mountain, so that the Chilean officials on the slope could only stand and gaze and salute it with their greetings.

I could see it plainly with the glass. Brilliantly illumined by our clinging searchlight, a crudely fashioned little flag. Stripes of red and white fabric; a field of blue, with stars!

I PUSHED MY way through the crowd of jabbering Chilean officials. A confusion of mingled Chileans and Americans. A glare of white lights. Banners flying; bugles blaring their mingled national salutes.

But the mountain—a mile in radius from this peak—was legally claimed for America!

I came upon Helga. Her outer robe was open. I saw beneath it her heavy red and blue cloak. Pieces of its cloth were cut from it.

"Joe!"

She flung herself into my arms. And then I saw Naina, standing with David, holding the rope from which their flag was flying.

She called to me.

Helga pushed me away. "We made the flag, Joe—cut it out of my cloak and Naina's white robe. And pinned it together. Go tell her how glad you are—our flag—her flag."

She pushed me. I stammered, "Hello, David. Naina, that flag—"

An international official had come with the Chilean expedition. He shoved his way toward us. His recorders, with their books, were at his elbow.

"Who raised this flag?" he demanded.

"I did," said Naina calmly.

"Who are you?"

"I am Naina, daughter of Judson Roberts of New York City. I was born in unclaimed, neutral Antarctica."

Her glowing eyes turned to David, and then came back to her questioner. Her voice rang clear:

"I am Naina Roberts. I claim this territory for the United States of America. I am an American!"

ABOUT THE AUTHOR

"HE IS A Verne returned and Wells going forward," remarked "Bob" Davis, dean of American magazine editors. "He is the American H.G. Wells," say other critics.

Cummings has an unusual flair for things scientific as evidenced by the fact that while at Princeton University he accomplished the remarkable feat of absorbing three years of physics in that many months. His five years' association with Thomas A. Edison as the latter's personal assistant also added to Cummings's scientific knowledge. His bizarre early life, living on orange plantations in Puerto Rico, striking oil in Wyoming, gold seeking in British Columbia, timber cruising in the North, before he was twenty, also left its imprint.

Leaving Mr. Edison's employ, Cummings began writing scientific fiction for many magazines. His stories gripped the popular imagination and they "clicked." Mr. Cummings's success as a writer has been meteoric, for in a few years he has become one of the world's most popular authors of scientific fiction.

Yet when asked about his own life and experiences Mr. Cummings is shy and evasive. He would much rather talk about Miss Betty Starr Cummings, his four-year-old daughter, whom he terms "the really interesting member of the family."

Ray Cummings

A few of her exploits include being wrecked and trans-shipped in a heavy sea; adrift with her parents in a disabled open boat when only three weeks old; traveling thousands of miles by automobile, train and steamer; weathering a Florida hurricane and coming safely through an automobile accident. From all of which we can see that Mr. Cummings leads rather an adventurous life himself!

Winter finds him at home in Bermuda, but when the temperature starts to rise he quickly makes tracks for Quebec. As we write this a letter arrives from Bermuda announcing that his next full length fantastic novel will soon be ready for *Argosy* readers.

In the office of *Fantastic Novels* the other day, Mr. Cummings looked this autobiography over with a smile. "It's all right," he said, "except that Betty is fourteen and has already sold a story of her own, which she wrote when she was thirteen. Fulton Oursler accepted it for *Liberty Magazine!*"

Asked about how he came to write "The Girl in the Golden Atom," Mr. Cummings said that it was the very first thing that he ever wrote, and that he did it simply because he felt like putting down and developing the idea of entering a world inside a ring. He had no thought of selling it, nor even that it might be a usable story. Two friends, William C. McNulty, an important American etcher, and

Spring Byington, motion picture actress (known nowadays as *the mother* in "The Jones Family" on the radio) looked over the story, and liked it. Mr. Cummings, who knew no rules for writing but simply put it down "straight from the heart" read it aloud to Mr. McNulty and to Miss Byington when either of them asked how it was coming along. They were very enthusiastic and urged him to take it to a publisher. Bob Davis snapped it up.

And Ray Cummings has been writing ever since.

www.ingramcontent.com/pod-product-compliance
Lightning Source LLC
Chambersburg PA
CBHW030531020726
47494CB00004B/1315